FEAR AND LOATHING IN LAS CRUCES

SHORT STORIES

JEFF BOWLES

Visit Jeff Bowles online:
Facebook at:
https://www.facebook.com/JeffRyanBowles
Twitter at: https://twitter.com/JeffBowlesLives
Tumblr at: http://authorjeffbowles.tumblr.com/
Amazon.com author page at:
https://www.amazon.com/Jeff-Bowles/e/B01L7GXCU0
YouTube's **Jeff Bowles Central** at:
https://www.youtube.com/channel/UC6uMxedp3VxxUC
S4zn3ulgQ

Printed in the United States of America
First Printing, March 2017

ISBN: 978-0-692-86038-0

TABLE OF CONTENTS

TO THE RISK TAKERS . . .

"It was sort of an ephemeral idea, as I understood it, distant and removed like the dark side of the moon or honest-to-God sobriety."

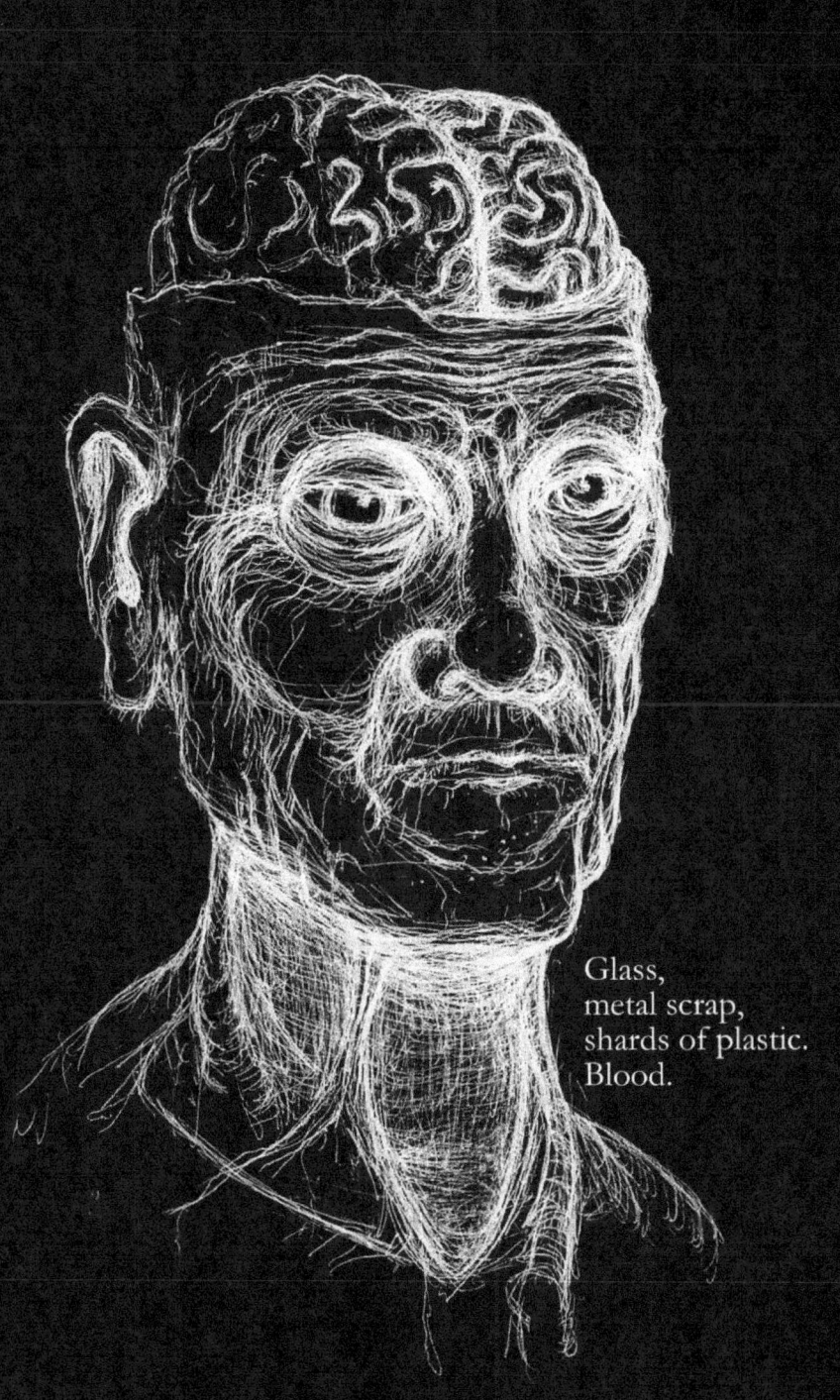

Glass,
metal scrap,
shards of plastic.
Blood.

FALCON HIGHWAY

Originally appeared in
the Hidden in Plain Sight anthology, November 2015

THEY came upon the wreck just after 2:00 AM. A forest green SUV, its front end mangled, totaled, the downed steel pole of a traffic light knifing through the engine. Ryan slowed the car as they approached, as he took the turn lane onto Falcon Highway.

"Jeez, it's a bad one," he said.

Lynn nodded in response.

Police and first responders gathered around the wreckage. Glass, metal scrap, shards of plastic. Blood. Ryan spotted it immediately, splattered on the windshield, as if it had been flung there to make for a convincingly grizzly scene. The ambulance was just

WILL OF THE WEST
(OR FEAR AND LOATHING IN LAS CRUCES)

CONSIDER, if you will, the sublimely totemistic Wild West Saloon. Replete with flowing libations, jangling piano, the rich, astringent scent of tobacco, poker games, showgirls, prostitutes....

Mmm. Prostitutes.

Clarence has really done me in this time. Before we left New York, I said to him, "Women? Beer? Whiskey? Women?"

He nodded and pursed his lips.

"You are aware, aren't you, that a man of my particular accomplishment has only four weaknesses in the entire world?"

"Four?" said Clarence. "You only listed three."

"Women count twice, Clarence. Women always count twice."

And it's true, you know. Women always count twice. Why I've got two right here, as a matter of fact. The comely sort, quite the lookers indeed. Each under employ, I've been told, of this fine establishment. The first sits on my lap, all snug and cozy like, preening and leering at me in all the right ways. The deep purple of her bodice and dress reminds me of succulent fruit, grapes fit to burst on the vine. She smells of apple butter, which may or may not, I realize, be the aroma of her perfume.

"Long Finger Willy," she says to me. "Why's that they call you Long Finger Willie anyhow?"

I smile at her, reach over and lace fingers with woman number two. A dark and raven-haired young thing. Hair might be dyed. Grin might be fake. Tell you what, though, the charm is 100% natural.

"You girls really want to know?" I say.

They nod at me and giggle.

"You really want to know why they call me Long Finger Willy?"

A hand lands on my shoulder. A brutishly large hand, though awfully primped and finefied. Dandy, you understand? I turn in my seat.

"Come now, Will," says the owner of that hand, "Why spoil everyone's afternoon? Don't you think you've got better stories to tell?"

That brutishly large hand, and that soft, pleasant, and yes, decidedly effeminate, voice. What a supreme time-waster, he is. What a joke of the modern age. A real turncoat bilker, an honest-to-God, ace-high murderer of a decent hog-killin' time. Sack o' monkey shit. Clarence really is a sack o' monkey shit.

"You're a real sack o' monkey shit, Clarence," I say.

Clarence shrugs. "Too bad I'm also your best friend, huh?"

"Yeah, too bad."

"Excuse us, ladies."

He takes me under the arm, pulls me to my feet. I sway a little, but not nearly as much as I have the right to. The girls, the women, they let out a simultaneous, "Awww."

"Duty calls, *ma cherries*. Jes lemme finish my drink," I say, throwing back my last little bit of whiskey. Slam the glass on the table, wipe my lips, smile at Clarence and say, "Where we headed, pal o' mine?"

Clarence leads me from the table. He gains an air of furtiveness, glances left, glances right.

"I think I've found our man," he says.

"Really? There's a man?"

"You know what I mean. A real desperado, an

honest range-rider. The old hell-rousing son of a gun who's going to show us the Will of the West."

The Will of the West. This is Clarence's pig to chase, certainly not mine. Imagine me, minding my own business in my little Lower East Side row house just about two months ago. Late morning sunlight poured in through the window, etching a luminous patchwork across my rough, splintered hard wood floor. I was doing my best to chase the old hair o' the dog; also doing my best to churn out as many pages of rip-roaring, spine-tingling action and abandon as was humanly possible. And in burst old Clarence to spoil the *humeur créative*. Old dour-pants Clarence, all talking about artistic credibility and verisimilitude and what-the-flaming-hell-have-I-been-doing-with-my-life.

"Our books are nonsense, Will," he said, pacing the floor. "Pure, unrepentant drivel. 'Cept I am repentant, now. I am. One cannot write about that which one does not know."

I blinked stupidly at him, eyes stinging and bleary, trying to decide if 11:29 in the A.M. was still technically too early for this sort of ballyhoo.

"But what about our novels?" I said. "What about White Mask McQuik?"

He threw his hands up. "White Mask McQuick! Pah! Novels! Ha! Dime novels. You understand, Will?

People only pay a flap-damn dime 'cause that's all they're flap-damn worth! I'm talking real literature, Will, work of honest significance. I'm talking, and hear me out here, I'm talking the Will of the West."

It was sort of an ephemeral idea, as I understood it, distant and removed like the dark side of the moon or honest-to-God sobriety. We'd know and understand this Will when we found it. We'd hear it calling to us, whispering across the desert sands in soft sagebrush rustling, yapping coyotes and whirling dust devils.

"What's this all about, Clarence?" I asked. "What the hell's gotten into you?"

Clarence paused. He scowled and reached into his coat.

"*This* is what's gotten into me," he said. "Terror, thy name is Western Union."

He slapped a little yellow piece of paper down on my desk, a telegram. And then Clarence spun on his heels and headed out the door.

The Western Union Telegraph Company
Sent: May 23, 1902

Boys—Latest White Mask McQuick sales numbers in. Dismal performance. Readership desires realism now. R-E-A-L-I-S-M. A whole stable of younger, cheaper talent lining up behind you. Make it real, or contracts terminated immediately.

Johan P. Beadle
Publisher, Johan & Co

*****

John-Michael Steele is ancient going on mother-gruffing old as hell. He leans into his saddle, as if his back cannot bear the weight of one more scorching Las Cruces day. His hair is long, ratty, has not seen the business end of a comb in days, has not seen the soap and suds of a bath in significantly longer. It is silver. Not gray, and certainly not without a bald patch or three. His weathered, mud-flecked duster is at least two sizes too large on his poor old willowy frame. He's got on a pair of genuine Confederate States cavalry boots. These boots are the only items about his person that are not dirty, torn, or otherwise beat all to hell.

I ask him how they came into his possession.

"Rode with General Jeb Stewart, I did," he says. His face twists into a sour sneer. Chewing tobacco drippings trail long and brown down his chin. "Rode with him through Fredericksburg and Chancellorsville and all the goddamn way to Gettysburg. Sure were a sad day when them fuckin' Yankee bags-a-piss won the war."

Clarence and I share a glance. Hmm, fuckin'

Yankee bags-a-piss. From one Yankee bag-a-piss to another, Clarence, I hope you're getting all the verisimilitude you can handle. We ride horseback on the long winding road from Las Cruces. The Organ Mountains rise high and pointed off to the east, and Picacho Peak to the northwest is a brown and knotted affair, sloping gently upward from cotton fields where migrant workers pick and pluck all day long. I reach into my pocket for my handkerchief, dab the sweat from my brow, eyeing now the harsh late-afternoon sun that lowers and lowers but never seems to go down.

"Mr. Steele," I pant, "how far exactly is it to this shaman we've heard so much about?"

John-Michael grumbles. His voice cracks when he speaks. "Never you mind jes how far it is. We get there when we get there. And don't call me Mr. Steele, neither. Mr. Steele was my grand-pappy. I look like a grand-pappy to you, green horn?"

Well, yes. Point of fact, that's exactly what you look like.

"Forgive my companion his crudeness, John-Michael," says Clarence. "I'm afraid heat makes him fussy."

"Fussy," says John-Michael. "Didn't reckon you two fellers'd be so talkative when you hired me. Didn't reckon you'd be so loquacious."

Clarence smiles. "Loquacious. Yes. Well, you see, we're both writers. Co-writers, that is, of a very successful series of novels."

John-Michael turns in his saddle, narrows his eyes at me, stares keen and long. He grumbles again.

"Novels?" he asks.

I nod. "Yes."

"What kinda novels?"

"Perhaps," says Clarence, "you've heard of the exploits of One-Eye Marie? Or, to discuss our most recent collaboration, perhaps you've heard of the adventures of White Mask McQuick?"

John-Michael twists up his face, snorts up some phlegm, and then cuts loose a large wad of tobacco and spit. The spit hits the leg of my horse, makes her flinch and nicker.

"You mean to tell me," says John-Michael, "that you're the writers of White Mask McQuick. Both'a you?"

"Yes, sir," says Clarence

"Them same little paper books we pay a dime for down at the general store?"

I nod and say, "The series is extraordinarily popular ... that is to say, the first few entries were."

John-Michael grins at this, and then he lets out the most raucous, wild peals of laughter I've ever heard from a gentleman of his advanced age. He snorts and he chortles. He brays like an ass, like a big, toothy, ratty-haired, old-as-all-hell ass.

Clarence and I glance at each other. I shrug. For his part, John-Michael goes on laughing and keening and generally making us feel like fools. Every once in a while, he'll gasp for breath and say things like, "Outhouse!" and "Asswipe!" Eventually, after the laughter has rocked his frail body for well over two minutes, he gasps one final time and gets it out.

"We use them books for asswipe in the outhouse!" he says. "*Asswipe* in the *outhouse*! You fellers! Aw Gawd, you fellers!"

Clarence's shoulders sag. He absentmindedly scratches at his nose. There really is nothing like being laughed at with wild abandon, is there Clarence? Verisimilitude. I try to think the word loud enough for Clarence to hear it.

Verisimilitude, Clarence. Verisimilitude.

*****

The sun finally dipped down below Apache Canyon about an hour and a half ago. As its last dying rays washed over the vast, forbidding New Mexican desert, we began riding into the foothills. John-Michael Steele lit a lantern, perched its ring on the barrel of a well-oiled 1858 Remington carbine. Flying ants and other local arthropoda danced and dove in and out of the lantern's light. A gentle breeze carried with it the scents of yucca flowers and lemony sage.

I turned once in my saddle to survey what we'd left behind. Las Cruces was there, twinkling away, soft and effervescent, glowing now from places like the train depot we first set foot in or the old saloon in which, I knew, still waited my perfect, leering prostitutes.

And so we rode into the night. We ride still. Clarence is still in search of this notion of his, and I … I suddenly do not doubt that unknown things can stir in the darkness. Perhaps it is some form of mystic charm. Perhaps it is majestic intent. The hairs on the back of my neck stand to full attention. A cold, clammy sweat beads on my brow, and I feel as though my senses are awakened and alive and grousing at me all at once.

John-Michael reins his horse to a sudden stop. He stiffens in his saddle, holds up a warning hand and glances back at Clarence and me. My own horse stumbles and halts, as does Clarence's. John-Michael unhooks the lantern from his carbine, and just for good measure, thumbs back the hammer with a harsh click and clack.

He raises the lantern high, calling into the night, "Who's there? By Gawd, who's there?"

There? Where? I didn't hear anything. Didn't see anything either. Clarence shakes his head. We both peer into the darkness.

"We know you're out there," says John-Michael. "Announce yerself now or so help me ..."

He doesn't finish the thought. And all there is to answer him, again, is stark, pressing silence.

The old Confederate cowboy raises his carbine, sets the butt against his shoulder, looks down the sights. He begins tracking something out there beyond the suddenly too-bright luminescence of his—

A gut-wrenching crack echoes in the night. John-Michael falls from his saddle. The lantern shatters. Gunshot. The light blinks out. I know it was a gunshot. I've written about that sound so many—

Someone shrieks at us. So near, so high and piercing. Someone? Or something? A desert creature? A monster, perhaps? A banshee's wail more than a shriek. And it is followed by another, to the right. And then another, far behind. And then it seems to me the entire New Mexico badlands erupt in shivering, trembling screams and moans and yelps and shrieking, shrieking, shrieking. Four dark figures rush at us from the brush. They drag Clarence from his horse. He hits the ground with a grunt. They do the same to me. The air rushes from my lungs. Someone stands over me, brandishing the carbine like a club.

"Holy Jesus!" I moan.

The carbine's stock slams into my temple.

*****

When consciousness returns to me, it does not do so gradually, but rather as a flood. I gasp awake. I am instantly aware of a campfire hissing and popping, of the taste of blood in my mouth. My hands are bound. My head feels as though a cargo train has rolled over it not once, not twice, but thrice.

"God, that smarts," I utter, licking the inside of my cheek.

"I know," utters a voice beside me, "dreadful, isn't it?"

Clarence is here with me, also with hands bound. And, like me, a crumpled heap slouching in the dirt.

"Clarence, thank Christ you're okay," I say.

"Yeah, you too, Will. Thank—"

"What have you done, Clarence? Mary the virgin, what have you done?"

Clarence blinks at me. "Done? Me?"

"You. What have you done?"

Clarence winces painfully. Blood and sweat run into his eye. "What's that supposed to mean?"

"Your trip, your adventure, your blasted will-of-the-what-the-shit."

He hisses, "Right. Right! As if I'm the one threating to terminate our contracts! As if I decided to kill John-Michael and get attacked by injuns."

"We ain't injuns, *gringo*."

Clarence and I freeze. It's now that I finally notice the fellow sitting across the fire from us. He is pudgy, cherub-like, or at least would be so, if he were not picking his teeth with a knife and pouring perfectly good tequila over a piece of bread. He slips the bread into his mouth and chews, never once, and with much apparent skill, removing the knife from that same orifice. He has a moustache and mocha skin. He is flanked by five others. They stand tall with arms folded, brandishing silver pistols and *bandolero* belts.

He plucks two more pieces of bread from a burnt little loaf. Douses them in tequila, tosses them to two of his *bandoleros*. The men grin at each other. One cocks his head in our direction, and the other chuckles. They come to our sides and take hold of us. Without a word, they shove the bread into our mouths.

"Now wait just a damn—" Flavor bursts in my mouth. Fruity, obnoxiously so. And also bitter, and also burning, and also burning, and also—holy flopsweat-suzie! Tastes like burning! Tastes like burn!

I cough and spit, as does Clarence. The bread, so saturated, so soaked it slid right down my throat. My eyes sting. What was that? Tears roll down my cheeks. That was no tequila.

"Name's Antonio, by the way," says the cherubic Mexican. "Pleased to meet'cha."

"Charmed," chokes Clarence, clearly unaware how ridiculous the response is.

The Mexican—Antonio—nods absentmindedly. He stares at us a few moments, and then his eyes light up and he snaps his fingers.

"Oh, yeah. Think I'm s'posed to tell you this. That cowboy you was with? He ain't dead. Winged the chicken-shit in the arm, the chicken-shit played dead awhile, then the chicken-shit up and skedaddled."

"Chicken-shit?" I say. "I mean, John-Michael?"

"*Hombre valiente!* Fucker just up and skedaddled."

I tongue the roof of my mouth. Wish I could lick it clean. Wish I could wash away, by means of my own spittle, that damn fruit and turpentine aftertaste.

"That wasn't tequila," I say. "What did you give us?"

Antonio smiles at this. He looks around at his *bandeleros*, who all snort and laugh.

"Yeah, that," says Antonio. "Well we'll get to that by-the-by."

He stands and walks around the fire. Antonio puts a hand under my chin, pushes my head left, pushes it right. He lets out a, "Hmph," and then moves to Clarence.

"Aye-aye-aye," he says, staring at Clarence's

bloodied forehead. "That must really sting."

Clarence spits out more blood. He glares at Antonio like he wants to gouge his eyes with spoon handles.

"It does, as a matter of fact," says Clarence, "and thanks so much for it, too. Now are you fellas going to kill us or are we just gonna chat all damn night?"

Antonio's gang seems to find this amusing. The snorting and chuckling continues.

"Kill you?" says Antonio.

Clarence nods.

"What makes you think we want to kill you?"

"You shot our guide and clubbed us unconscious," I say.

"Yeah, but that doesn't mean … Wait, *Madre de dios*. You mean you two don't know?"

Clarence and I stare at each other.

Antonio laughs. "You mean you honestly do not know?"

"Know what?" says Clarence.

And that's about when I start feeling queer. Comes on at first like a rumbling in my guts. Like I'm about to have the backdoor trots, or what have you. But then the rumbling subsides, and becomes more of a … warmth.

"Boys, gentlemen, that whole thing, it was just an act!" Antonio declares.

"Act?" says Clarence.

The warmth in my stomach builds, grows, sort of spreads out, up into my arms and down my legs.

"Sure, I winged that old cowboy good, but it's no worse than the boss told me to do," says Antonio.

Clarence shakes his head. "Boss?"

"You really don't know, huh? Boys, I am under employ of Johan Beadle. We all are."

Johan Beetle? What's a Johan Beetle? God, I feel strange.

"Johan Beadle," says Antonio. "You know, *your publisher? Madre de Dios!* This is all just a misunderstanding! He hired us to come out here and look all tough and rough you up and such and such."

Clarence snorts, his mouth agape. Why's he look so straight when I feel so...? No, I can tell he's feeling it, too, that same warmth in his guts, in his arms and legs and in his face. He's starting to sweat and get all twitchy just like me. That warmth is all-encompassing now. And really, if you're gonna feel warmth throughout your corporeal-self entire, this'd be the kind of warmth you'd most want to feel. Kind of pleasant, actually, kind of … funny.

I start laughing. Not really sure why. Just start laughing.

"What the hell's so funny?" says Clarence.

And then Clarence starts giggling. No one seems

more surprised than him. Giggling turns to laughter, and then old Clarence, he starts cackling like a crazy person. I've never found anything so funny. All of us laugh, even Antonio and his *bandoleros*. Heh heh. Real, real pretty. And funny. So damn funny it hurts.

Antonio stumbles over to cut our bonds.

"C'mon," someone says, "maybe the Will of the West is over in that gulley."

"Will? But that's my name. Or Long Finger Willie, if you prefer."

"Couldn't rightly call it the Long Finger Willie of the West, *pendajo*," says Antonio. "Just wouldn't be proper."

Golly, he's pretty. Like a little rainbowy Mexican confection. I follow Antonio and Clarence and the *bandoleros* down to the gully. The gully is dry, but very, very colorful.

"Holy gypsum!" I shout. "What in the hell did you feed us, Antonio?"

"Fed you bread, now didn't I?"

"Antonio! Antonioooooooo!"

"That wasn't just bread," says Clarence. "What was it? Am I dying? Am I dead?"

"Antonio! Clarence is dyyyyyeeeeing!"

"No, he ain't," says Antonio. He strips off his shirt and motions for us all to do the same. We do it, without question, because it seems right.

"Nobody's dying," he says. "Everybody's safe. What'd I give you? Fire mescal."

"Wait," says Clarence. "Mescal? Where have I heard that before?"

"Peyote, *pendajo!* I gave you both peyote liquor! You wanna find the Will of the West? You gotta do it just like the Injuns. I have no eyes! I have no eyes! *Madre de dios*, I have no goddamn eyes!"

"Are these them?"

"Yes. Ouch. Thanks for pointing them out. Ouch."

By-the-by and after a while, we all lay sprawled out around the fire. The flames have nearly burned themselves out, but the heat they provide compliments very nicely the warmth still wriggling and writhing its way throughout my body. We talk about things. Great, weighty, important things. Sometimes it's hard, and sometimes Antonio and his *bandoleros* speak in long streams of indecipherable Spanish. But we feel good. Least I do. I feel just about all sorts of all right.

"Fellas?" I say. "I love you all so much."

That's when I spot her. Standing there just beyond the flickering firelight. I don't ask who she is or where she came from. I do not bother pondering why she's here or, for that matter, if she's real or some kind of fevered vision.

But yes, she is there. Beckoning me. The single most beautiful creature I have ever seen. Long, lithe, supple legs. Round, promising, mesmeric hips. Breasts. Perfect, bare breasts for me to have because she wants me to have them. The hair is the color of a Las Cruces sunset. The scent—for I can smell her from here—is much better than perfume or apple butter or anything the vague notion of woman or prostitute can conjure or produce. Know what it smells like? Really want to know? Smells like the top of a newborn's head. Smells like a baby. Like a perfect, cooing, gorgeous little baby. And I am a baby in her presence. I am born again, born anew. I have never existed before this moment, and as far as I can see, I shall never exist hence, save in her radiance and beauty.

I don't excuse myself from the group. I simply stand and walk. I take one, long, savoring footstep after another. I cross to her like she is a golden goddess, promised, from on holy high, to meek, flawed man. And when I make it to her, and when I lay my hands on her breasts, and when I kiss her deep and true, that's when I know.

This woman right here? She does not count twice. She does not count thrice. She does not, to be sure, count a fourth, fifth, or sixth time. She counts once. Only once and a perfect once. We make love in the desert, as the coyotes yip and the stars shine on us, just as they must shine on all God's creatures.

*****

I wake up feeling like a dog turd. Like a trained chimp all shat out with no more tricks to show. Tongue is sewn to the roof of my mouth. Taste buds feel like overused sandpaper. I groan in pain. Head hurts like the dickens; reach down to scratch myself.

I am buck nude. Not a scrap of cloth in sight. And I'm in the desert. And there are signs of a recently pitched camp. And I am all alone. Wasn't I with people?

"Wasn't I with Clarence?" I say.

A hand lands on my arm. A brutishly large hand, though awfully primped and finefied. Dandy, you understand? It squeezes. I turn my head. Clarence is here. And Clarence is nude. And I am nude. And Clarence is nude. And we are nude together.

Together? Wasn't there a together last night?

Last night?

I shriek. I push Clarence away and jump to my feet and start hopping around till all the little rocks and pebbles cut up my feet. Clarence groans.

"Holy Jesus!" I say.

Clarence groans again.

I say, "Holy Jesus!"

He opens his eyes and takes in the situation all at

once. The nudeness. The crudeness. The ... the last night. He jumps to his feet as well.

"Holy Jesus!" he says.

"Holy Jesus!" I shriek.

*****

The train ride back to New York is long and, most graciously, quiet. I say two words to him the whole time. He says less than two back. At Grand Central Depot in beloved New York City, we stand facing each other, jaws clenched and arms folded tight. Passengers and arrivers and departers surge around us, concerned only with their own comings and goings. A gentle rain is falling out in the train yard. The smell of early summer showers comes to us, yet it does nothing at all to soothe or revitalize.

I am the first to speak, but I do not envy myself the task. "So, erm, I'll call on you later next week, shall I?"

Clarence nods. "Yes, that would be sensible. Still have a lot more tidying up to do in chapter five."

"Yes, erm, chapter five. And don't forget chapter seven."

"Yes, can't forget about chapter seven."

"Erm, yes."

"Yes."

"Erm…"

We stand there a few moments longer. Moments?

Ah, hell. Guess it could be hours, days, weeks, months, years.

"Will," Clarence finally says. "Are we all right? As friends? You know, as best friends?"

I think about this for a time. "Yes, I believe so. It's a crazy old world, you know? Just a funny, funny old world. For instance, do you want to know how I got the name Long Finger Willy?"

"Stop right there," Clarence says. "Never shall another word be spoken. What happens in Las Cruces, Will...."

"What happens in Las Cruces stays in Las Cruces."

ACKNOWLEDGMENTS

Many thanks to the people who've gotten me this far. Educators, peers, family and friends. You know who you are. Sometimes life can be a bumpy ride. Then again, so can the road to Las Cruces....

now pulling onto Highway 24. A policeman watched it leave, stuffing a wadded and bloodied red flannel shirt into a plastic bag.

"Maybe we should stop," said Lynn.

Ryan stared at the shirt a moment and then looked at Lynn. She was still pale, looked exhausted. She still had on the medical bracelet, the one they'd issued her in the emergency room.

"Babe, it's been a hell of a night," he said. "I think we ought to get you home."

"Just stop and ask."

"Babe, I don't—"

"Stop and ask, Ryan. Maybe we can help."

Ryan sighed at her, but all the same, he pulled to a stop and rolled down his window. The nearest police officer—tall, neat, sagging gut—came to the driver's side and leaned in.

"Something I can help you folks with?" he said.

Ryan smiled at him. "Just wondering if there's anything we can do."

The officer turned to look at the departing ambulance. "I'm afraid there's not much to do. Just another speed demon on Falcon Highway."

Falcon, Colorado, fourteen miles to the northeast of Colorado Springs, home to 11,000 residents and growing all the time. Most of those residents—most of the new ones, anyway—lived in the subdivisions and suburbs on the north end, but the oldest parts of the far-flung community, the parts that'd been converted from farmland and sectioned off into rural subdivisions, they could only be accessed by Falcon Highway: two lanes, twenty miles long, blind hill after blind hill.

Ryan and Lynn had only lived in Falcon a few years, but they knew the reputation the road had earned. The dozen or so little wooden crosses that stood scattered along its length, the horrific night many years ago when the prom queen had been ejected from her car and had landed, face first, thirty yards away in the dirt. Ryan thought he understood the officer's casual smile. Fatalities on this road were nothing new.

"Thanks for stopping, though," said the officer. "Most people just blow right past."

Ryan nodded at this. "No problem. Have a good night."

"Likewise. You folks watch yourselves out there. Weatherman says there may be fog tonight. Whenever there's one wreck on Falcon Highway, the second isn't too far behind."

They pulled away and left the police and first responders. Twelve miles to home, twenty-five minutes or so if Ryan obeyed the speed limit. Very few people traveled the road at this time of night. The head lamps only barely illuminated the highway, as if light was a commodity for which the darkness was a miser.

They drove on in silence for a period of time longer than Ryan felt comfortable with. He knew he should talk to Lynn. He should ask how she felt, if she was in pain. Instead, all he could manage was a vague and mumbled, "Doughnuts."

"What?" said Lynn.

"It's Sunday now. After we get some sleep, we should go back into town and get some doughnuts."

"Oh. Okay."

"You like doughnuts. You know, glazed and chocolaty and gooey. Doughnuts."

"Yes," she said, "I'm familiar with the concept."

He chuckled, but even he knew it had no soul to it. For her part, Lynn gave a meek smile.

"Ry?" she asked.

"Yeah?"

"We get along, don't we? I mean, we're doing okay, right?"

"I should hope so. That ring wasn't exactly the cheapest—"

"I want to try again."

Ryan paused. He studied her face to see if she was on the verge of tears again. She wasn't.

"We don't really want to think about this right

now." He wasn't asking; he was telling.

"I do," Lynn said. "I think it's the perfect time to think about it."

"Babe, you've had a hard night. We both have. I mean we just lost our ... we just had—"

"A miscarriage. We lost our baby."

Ryan's breath caught in his throat. Lynn was a lot of things, but she wasn't normally so blunt.

"Right," he said, though he suddenly found it difficult to look her in the eye. They crested a low hill, the first of many to come. Just as they reached its bottom, headlights appeared in Ryan's rear-view mirror. Funny, he hadn't seen them a moment ago.

"Get back on that horse," said Lynn. "That's what my Dad would have to say about it."

"Horse? Lynn, this isn't a race."

"Isn't it? I mean, we aren't getting any younger."

In the mirror, the headlights grew larger. Ryan glanced at his speedometer. He was doing forty-five. This guy must've been doing sixty at least.

"I know we aren't," said Ryan. "I just think, under the circumstances, we ought to maybe sleep on it."

"I guess. It's just that tonight I thought ... well, I don't feel very good. It hurts kind of a lot, and I just want to think about making this whole thing work for us."

The headlights were upon them now, following so

closely Ryan had the sudden urge to speed up.

"You're stronger than me," said Lynn. "I know it isn't hitting you as hard, but—"

"Are you seeing this?"

It had to be a truck, locked into its high beams, glaring and filling Ryan and Lynn's car with harsh yellow light. The truck swerved. It knifed into the west-bound lane, drifted slowly back, knifed again. Its horn blared, long and sustained, followed by a rapid burst of punctuated honks.

"Who the hell does this guy think he is?" said Ryan.

"An idiot. Just let him pass."

"So he can go on thinking he's not an asshole?"

They'd seen this kind of driving more times than Ryan could remember. Something about a wide-open country road, it made people careless, overconfident. He was in no mood to get pushed around, not right now. He pumped his breaks.

"Get off my ass," he said. And then he rolled down his window, stuck his hand out, and flipped the bird. The driver stayed on them, honking obnoxiously, glued to their bumper.

"Oh, well done," said Lynn. "You sure showed him. Just let it go. Or do you want to make us accident number two?"

Ryan slammed on his breaks. Tires squealed. The

truck swerved, but in one smooth motion, it righted itself. A long, sustained honk, and then it sped up. It got beside them. Not a truck at all, Ryan realized. An SUV, forest green, just like the one in the wreck. He tried to get a glimpse inside the cabin, but the windows were tinted black. The SUV nimbly passed them, and then it sped off, disappearing over a hill, leaving Ryan and Lynn alone on the open road.

"Was that really necessary?" said Lynn.

Ryan didn't answer.

"You could have gotten us killed."

"Jerk had to be taught a lesson."

"I don't get you. You say you want to get me home—in one piece, I assume—and then you pull a stunt like that."

They began to climb the hill.

"Don't start," said Ryan. "I'm not in the mood."

"You think I am?"

"This isn't about you."

"Oh? And I suppose it's actually about ... Ow."

Lynn pressed her hand against her abdomen. She uttered a curse and sucked in hard through her teeth.

"You okay?" he asked.

"It hurts again."

Her face paled. Her breathing became ragged. She put a hand down into the crotch of her jeans, let it rest there a few moments, and then raised it back up.

A streak of fresh blood ran from her index finger and over her thumb.

Ryan's stomach lurched. "Let me turn around, get you back to the hospital."

"Home," said Lynn. "Take me home."

"Sweetie, I don't think—"

"The doctor said this might happen. Just need ... need a fresh pad."

They crested the hill. A flat, rolling landscape spread out below them, the twinkling of houselights now visible on the horizon. The taillights of the SUV were closer than Ryan expected. Another car approached in the opposite lane.

"Doughnuts," said Lynn.

"Huh?"

The SUV neared the oncoming car, which was smaller and lower to the road, some kind of sports car.

"What kind of doughnuts ... should we get?" said Lynn.

"Sprinkled," Ryan said. "And maybe some glazed, too."

The SUV swerved. It cut to the left of the sports car, missed it narrowly on the road's shoulder. Tires squealed. The car turned sharply, lifted off its passenger-side tires, stopped dead on its driver-side tires, and then it flipped, one side and then the other.

Smashed glass and twisted metal. It flipped again, landed on its top, skidded off the road into a ditch.

"Jesus," said Lynn.

The SUV honked its horn. It righted itself back into the east-bound lane, and then once again, drove off down Falcon Highway.

Ryan sped down the road to the spot the car had flipped and pulled onto the shoulder.

"Call 911," he said.

"I can't."

"Why not?"

"Think about where we are."

Cell phones on Falcon Highway. Coverage this far out from the Springs was spotty, even at the best of times. Ryan reached into his pocket for his phone. No signal.

"Stay here," he said.

He got out. There, in the ditch, the sports car lay on its top. It was an older model, bright yellow, early '90s by the look of it. The fender was horribly bent out of shape, nearly all the windows shattered. One bright white taillight hung from its housing, still rocking back and forth on its wires.

"Are you okay in there?" Ryan called. "We're gonna get you some help."

He approached slowly. A cloud of dust hung in the air, stinging his nostrils. Ryan bent beside the driver's window. It was smashed, but largely intact. He reached for his phone, activated its flashlight ... There was no one in the car. No one behind the wheel, the passenger seat was completely empty.

He swept his eyes over the field. No blood, no clothing, no marks in the dirt. Where had the driver gone? Ryan bent closer. There, dangling from the rearview mirror, was a graduation tassel. Green and gold, the colors of Falcon High School. '93, it read.

Confused, Ryan made his way back to Lynn. He opened his door and sat behind the wheel.

"Well?" Lynn asked.

"I don't know. There wasn't...."

"Wasn't what?"

"There wasn't ... anybody. Nobody was driving that thing."

"What do you mean?"

Ryan shrugged. "I looked around. I couldn't find anyone."

"You were only there a minute."

"I looked, damn it. Nobody was driving that car."

Lynn stared at him, an odd expression clouding her features. Was it disbelief? Fear? Or was she disappointed in him?

"Well we need to go back into town so we can call someone," she said.

"What we need is to get you home. We'll call from

there."

"Why would I need to go—"

He reached for her wrist, held up her hand. Her eyes drifted to it, lingered on the blood there. He fastened his seatbelt, motioned for her to do the same. She didn't. He frowned at her, but understood it'd do no good to pester. Ryan threw the car into gear and pulled back onto the road.

Lynn eyed him. They sped past mile marker six, fields of freshly reaped grass pulled into dark bundles on either side of them.

"I don't think you get to decide like that," she said.

He didn't answer.

"Hello? There's someone lying dead in a field back there and you just want to ignore it."

"Not open for discussion, not from you," Ryan said.

"What is that supposed to mean?"

"It means, my loving wife, that this has been the shittiest night of our lives. And guess what? It isn't getting any better. We're going home, you're going to bed, and once I'm sure you aren't in pain anymore, *I* will call 911."

Lynn had no response for this. She opened her mouth, shut it again, glanced at the road ahead. "Well we're not going anywhere fast in that fog."

"What fog?"

It appeared out of nowhere, thick and impenetrable, completely obscuring the road ahead. It pressed in around their car, rendering the high beams useless. Ryan had seen sudden fog on Falcon Highway before, but this was ridiculous. He'd had a mind to speed home, more or less so he could tell Lynn he was doing everything he could. But now, urgency seemed like the worst idea on a night full of worst ideas. He eased off the gas, slowing down until the speedometer's needle settled on twenty-five.

Their lights cut out. Not just the headlights, but the dashlights, too. They plunged into darkness. Lynn gasped. He slammed on his breaks, stopping in the middle of the highway.

He said, "Are you okay?" and then he heard a strange smacking sound, right there in the backseat. It was wet, loud. Their lights flared back to life. He looked in the rearview mirror. There, behind his wife, sat a young woman. A teenage girl, sporting a pink satin dress, a sparkling tiara, and the kind of hairdo he hadn't seen since he was a kid. Half her face was gone, completely torn off. Blood dripped onto the dress, gore clinging to her exposed skull. Her jaw was disconnected on one side. It flapped open and closed, even as she fed herself a chocolate doughnut.

Ryan shrieked. He spun around. No one there.

Lynn said, "What?"

His heart hammered in his chest. The strangest thoughts occurred and the feeling of blind terror like an open wound.

"What is it, Ry?"

His eyes darted over the backseat. Lynn took hold of him, shook him. His eyes snapped to hers. Whatever Lynn saw in them, whatever primal force, it must not have seemed like him at all.

"What did you see?" she asked.

"Home ... We need to go."

"Why? What is it?"

He drew away from her. "I'm tired. It's late and it's been a shit night. I'm just, I need to get some sleep. It's getting to me."

"What do you mean? What's getting to you?"

"I wanted it. You would not believe how bad I wanted it, Lynn."

"Come on, honey, focus on me."

"The baby. I really wanted the—"

Two beams of light flared to life at the top of the hill. Yellow, striking and fierce.

"What the hell is that?" said Lynn.

They shone on in isolated stillness, filtered through the fog, catching water particles, haloed and lording, the light at the end of the tunnel. A horn blasted. The engine revved and the SUV sped down at them.

"Ryan?"

"I see it."

"Ryan!"

He cranked the wheel and punched the gas, but it was too late. The SUV slammed into them head-on. Ryan shot forward, was instantly pulled pack. The front end crumpled, the steering wheel mashed into his testicles. The car skittered on its wheels. Ryan's head went full-force into the driver's side window.

Everything rocked and jolted a few moments, and then all became still.

He groaned, felt the pain like knives gouging his scalp, thudding hammers smashing his testicles. What was that sound? A smacking noise. And there, with just the faintest wisp tickling his nose, the rich scent of chocolate frosting.

He opened his eyes. Lynn was no longer beside him. She was draped over the dashboard, kneeling in place on the carpeted floor. Her head had gone through the windshield. She never put on her seatbelt. More blood, not just on her fingers. Ryan couldn't tell if she was breathing or not.

The smacking in the backseat stopped. He had to save his wife. The green SUV had suffered damage, but it was heavier, tougher. He recognized it could still be driven.

His head numb and cut, his balls broken, he opened his door and fell to the asphalt. Smells of the

Falcon prairielands greeted him. Dusty, dry, a punch of wildflowers, like he'd inhaled some, like they were everywhere in the blackness. Ryan climbed to his feet, pulled himself up by the side-view mirror. He limped to the driver's side of the SUV, peered in, surprised to find no one behind the wheel. He limped back to the car, wrapped his arms around Lynn's waist and pulled her from the jagged glass of the windshield. It cut her face. There was nothing he could do about it.

He had a mind to sling her over his shoulder, but he was too weak. He had to drag her instead, body rife with agony, screaming to the night and the gentle prairie breeze. Somehow he got her to the SUV, lifted her, slung into the passenger seat.

Where was he now? Six miles down Falcon highway, six from the police and first responders. Another six miles to home. East or west? He chose home, east. The keys were still in the ignition. He got in and turned the engine over, threw the SUV in reverse, spun it around, threw it into drive.

Ryan did sixty in the fog. Five miles to home. Now four. Lynn gurgled beside him. She was breathing.

"Hang in there, babe," he murmured.

Three miles to home. Two miles.

There it was again, that smacking sound. The chew, chew, chew of a flapping jaw on doughnuts. He glanced into the mirror. The ruined girl from the class of '93 grinned at him. And there was someone else beside her, a balding man in a red flannel shirt. His skull was split down the middle. Both of them enjoyed their doughnuts. The girl spoke without speaking.

You just drive on ahead, she said. *As soon as you're dead, I'll make you my prom date.*

May I have another? said the balding man.

Oh, yes, please do. Whenever there's one wreck on Falcon Highway, the second ain't too far behind.

One mile to home. Ryan blinked at the razors in his mind, adjusted himself to his smashed and throbbing balls. He told himself not to turn around. There would be nobody behind him. Just like before.

Half a mile, that was all.

The prom queen and her bald victim noshed and said things like *mmm* and *nummy*. Was that a doughnut? It was bloody and small. Was it ... a fetus? Ryan shrieked. Dear lord, were they eating a fetus? Was it his? Were they eating his baby? He shrieked again. Lynn was still breathing. Still time to have another baby, to live and love and be happy together.

He almost missed it, Peerless Farms, the road through their subdivision. He drew closer, ignored the smacking in the back seat, prepared to turn. The fog lightened, and then, all at once, it disappeared.

Ryan suddenly found himself in the turn lane of

Highway 24 onto Falcon Highway, twelve miles and twenty minutes back in the opposite direction, the beginning of the entire road. He blinked stupidly at the red traffic light swaying on its cabling. There, off to the side, a terrible car wreck, forest green SUV smashed all to hell. No police were there, no first responders. Ryan felt himself crumble to the madness of it.

Very few people traveled the road at this time of night. The head lamps barely illuminated the highway ahead, as if light was a commodity for which the darkness was a miser.

Ouch, said the prom queen. *Tough luck, buddy. You just drive on ahead. We'll get ya sooner or later. We can do this all night, you know what I mean?*

May I have another doughnut? said the bald man with the split skull.

Oh, yes. Yes, please do, replied the girl, her voice rabid like the death of babies.

"The truth is many of my possessions are beyond my reckoning...."

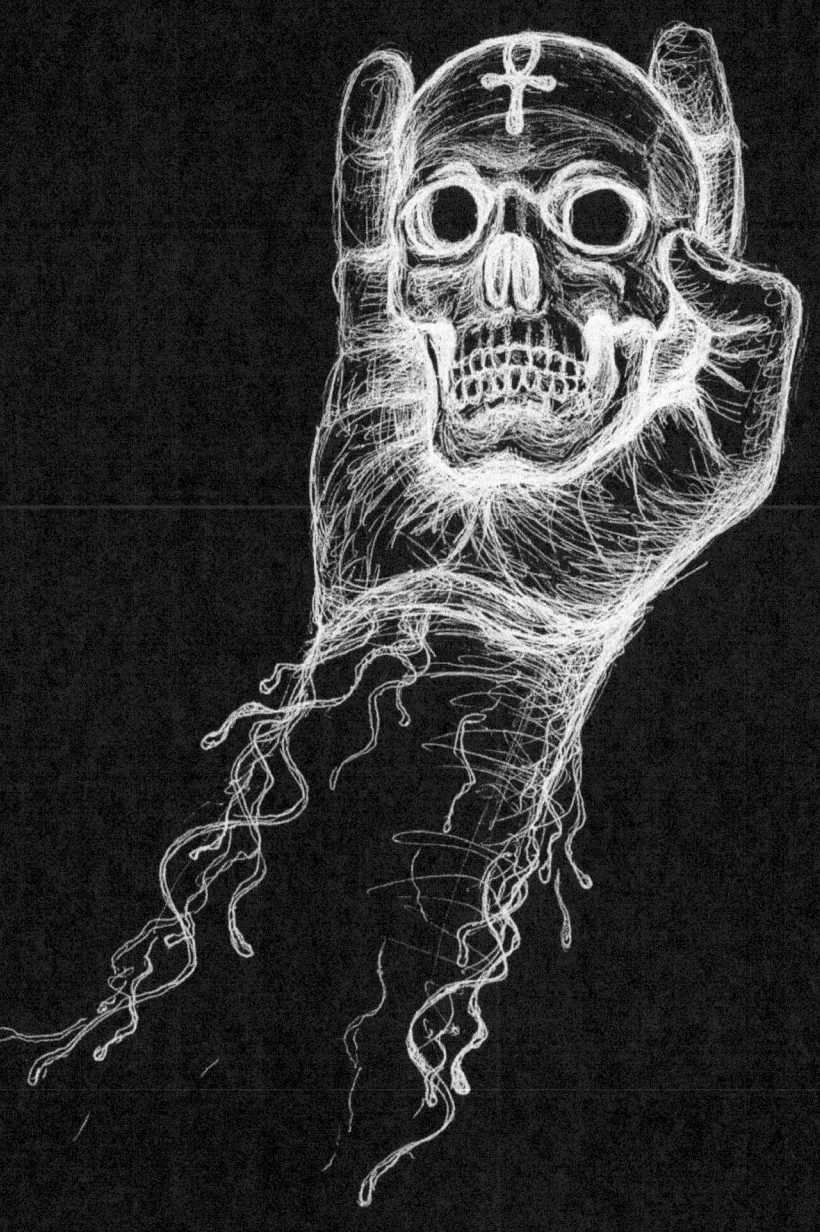

THE DEAD MAN'S HAND

JASON had been dead some forty-three years before John Kayce invited him into his employment. By definition, the dead served the living, and Jason was the best Eye available, so it seemed natural to receive Kayce's Dead Man's Hand, an energetic black calling card which meant Jason's contract had been reacquired. Granted the go ahead by the local ghostly affairs agency, Jason arrived at Kayce's palatial home on a foggy and still January night, the precise time and date of which eluded him. He wore no watch and understood hours and minutes in a manner befitting a ghost, which was to say, not very well at all.

The house was large, purple and snow-swept, the moon overhead showering the lawn in shades of indigo and blue. A well-kept winter garden stretched from the walkway to the front door, an assortment of lawn ornaments and covered flower beds a sure sign the lady of the house managed more visual expression than did the man. Little was known of Belladonna Kayce, who was by all accounts a recluse. Jason had asked the dead girl at the agency exactly what John did for a living. She'd given him a rather strange and indefinite answer. The psych system listed he dealt in artifacts of the nether realms, a bit of nonsense Jason didn't understand. There was no such thing, not as far as he knew.

In a sea of pain and etheric miasma, receiving the gift of life and then expiring sometime thereafter meant agony without end, for when an individual died, he or she became enslaved for an extended period determined by that flowing universal energy some referred to as God. Which made little sense to sentient beings and followed its own strange habits and omnipresent discourse.

Jason checked his pockets for his Dead Man's Hand, ensuring his energetic papers were in order. He passed beyond the gated entrance and floated along the cobblestone path to the front door, opened his mind and reached for the man who'd sent for him.

Mr. Kayce. Jason DeMont here. I've come as your new Eye.

A slight pause followed, and then a disembodied

voice flooded his being. *Ah yes, Mr. DeMont. How nice of you to come. You'll find the premises quite unguarded. Meet me in my lab, won't you?*

Jason nodded and passed not through the door but rather condensed his incorporeal being and fit himself inside the small leather tube nested beside the black mailbox. Leather was a natural conductor of spiritual energy. Having once been alive itself, it was also a very fine transcription device. For all in the realm of the dead, leather acted as road signs and maps, point-to-point transit systems which could be imprinted with precise coordinates. Jason found inside the tube exact directions to Kayce's lab. He thought to move in that direction and traveled.

In a flash of light, he found himself in a large room full of collected lithographs, paintings, arcane objects, books, and indeed, artifacts. He recognized few of them, though each owned a nametag. Rather than being unkempt or messy, the room was tidy, well-ordered. Old portraits hung on the walls, depictions of individuals most likely deceased themselves. John Kayce was clearly a man of affectation and long memory. The room sent a chill through Jason's being, though such a sensation was common amongst objects of use and age.

He spotted the man himself bent over a long table full of handguns, spear heads, and cannonballs. If indeed these artifacts belonged to some nether realm beyond Jason's, it must've been a strange and startlingly physical place.

"I feel your presence, my friend," Kayce said, never taking his eyes from the table. "Allow me a moment to collect my spectacles and I'll be right with you."

The living, of course, couldn't see ghosts with the naked eye. They needed help, so Kayce went to a set of drawers in the far corner beneath a large stuffed peacock and a white albatross. John rummaged through them as Jason allowed himself to float freely. He approached what appeared to be a sheet of severely degraded papyrus, rolled over in scroll fashion. It contained some brown scratches, hieroglyphics. He marveled at it and reached a ghostly hand to touch it. The papyrus fluttered and glowed a malevolent blue. A projected image sprang from it, two hawks picking to death a body in ancient sands. Jason gasped.

Kayce spun around. "Don't touch that!"

Jason recoiled, feeling an odd sense of vertigo. "Apologies, sir. I didn't mean to disturb your work."

"Yes, well you would be sorry if you understood the significance. Above all else, my ghastly friend, you are not to touch anything in this house unless you have my permission. Very many objects here have been imprinted by forces you wouldn't comprehend. No one's going to rescue you if you end up in ancient Giza, turn of the century Chicago, or anywhere else for that matter."

Kayce harrumphed and slid his spectacles onto his face. He blinked a few times and took the measure of Jason, looking him up and down. Jason wondered how he appeared, himself never having seen a ghost in life. Jason had died so terribly young. His age, in fact, was often the first thing clients commented on. Drowned in the pool over summer vacation. A client might pry or feign concern, but of course, it was far too late for him, and as a general rule, the living cared little for the dead.

Thankfully, Kayce made no such comments. He merely pushed the spectacles up his nose and said, "You're fully qualified, I expect. The agency would never send someone ill equipped."

"I am, though I'm curious why you need the services of an Eye. What are these artifacts you collect, Mr. Kayce? What just happened?"

"Too many questions already, my friend. I'll enquire first, if you don't mind. Firstly, where do you hail from?"

"Massachusetts."

"That's not what I meant. Your family, are there any seers? You have a long line of spectral attachment, I expect?"

Jason stood taller. "I don't, actually, the first of my line. My family is still alive, and none of them can see me."

"Hmph. That must have made things difficult when you crossed over."

"Somewhat, sir. I've never shirked from my duties. On the contrary, you'd be hard pressed to find a better Eye."

Kayce's brow lifted. "Boasting. How unbecoming."

"Not at all. I simply know my worth."

John cocked his head and began pacing the room. He raised a finger and traced it along the contour of a large blue marlin hanging on the wall. It seemed at first to be an ordinary fish, yet the more Jason focused on it, the more he felt it thrum with energy.

"Do you know what this is?" Kayce asked. Jason shook his head.

"Neither do I. The truth is many of my possessions are beyond my reckoning. I've managed to collect them by sense alone, but as you well know, the sight of a dead man is much keener. It's why I need an Eye, you understand?"

Jason stumbled over his words. "I-I'm afraid I don't. This is not a matter of far-seeing? Spiritual protection, astral projection, things of that nature?"

"No, I've no use for parlor tricks, my friend," Kayce said. "You've little choice in how you serve the living. That much we both understand. Come here and touch this for me."

Jason hesitated. A low cry seemed to emanate from his throat, though he himself made no noise. He moved to the marlin, and as his fingers met its lacquered scales, a projection spilled forth. On the dock of some long-ago peer, where nearby children in homespun woolen garb laughed and played, an old fisherman cast his line into frigid waters. Though the projection was a solid, pallid green, Jason could sense the fisherman was drunk and rather depressed.

The fisherman thought to himself, *Well Bart, that's the last straw, innit? How'll I ever get Margaret back? Gave me her hand and then wrenched it away. And all I've got left is me cards.*

The man was a gambler, then, and a poor one at that. He pulled a flask from his coat, had a long, stiff belt, and then cast his line too hard and fast. Bart slipped, hit his head on the peer and rolled into the water. The children spotted him as he went under and scrambled to go find help. None came in time. The man drowned much as Jason had.

Jason wrenched his hand away as a terrible chill spread through his being. The projection disappeared, leaving him cold and terrified.

"A strange artifact to be sure. Are you all right, my friend?" Kayce said.

Jason nodded. Myriad questions entered his mind, but he didn't need to utter them. Kayce seemed to guess his line of thinking.

"I had to be sure," he said. "Yes, you've some talent, that much is certain. The projection leapt to meet you, a rarity in my experience. You ask what I do for a living. My trade is in the collecting and reselling of tragedy. The nether realms are made of tragedy. Specifically, these objects you see here were all on or about individuals who died and who have not, as far as anyone can tell, crossed over."

"You mean…"

"They're still alive, in some manner of speaking," John said. "Or at least, they aren't precisely what you'd call deceased. If you like, you may think of me as a curator of these realms, those places and times which have now slipped beyond us."

"Mr. Kayce, that was rather … difficult for me."

"Of course it was. It isn't easy work. Tell me, my friend, if you come from ordinary stock, how is it you possess such ability? You must have died rather tragically yourself. How did you expire? And why is it you look so young?"

Jason was 17 when he drowned, and the memory of it was fresh as the day it happened. His parents—

the affluent sort—threw a rowdy party one July evening which he and a few friends had snuck into. Just like the fisherman, young Jason had developed a taste for liquor, so the circumstances of his death were similar enough the thought of pursuing this contract further made him swoon.

"I accept on one condition," he said. "If at any time I become lost in one of these nether realms …"

"You won't," said Kayce. "I understand the laws of psychic protection and energetic transmutation better than anyone. Plenty of barriers exist in this room and indeed throughout the entire house. My wife is also very capable. I think you'll find her a bit of a bruiser when it comes to dealing with your ghastly sort, if you don't mind the expression."

"I don't. I also don't believe you. To be blunt, Mr. Kayce, you are a silly, stubborn man if you think no harm can befall either of us for dabbling in arcane magic. The very fact these artifacts exist in their current state suggests a soul trap or some other means of banned metaphysics. We aren't dealing in child's play. There is a very real, very natural component to all of this. Nobody gets between a man and his fate without consequences."

John waved away his misgivings. "But of course. I know all that. This is not my first time, you know. Dear boy, I've been dealing in such things for decades. You have no idea to whom you're speaking, do you? I put the paranormal antiquities trade on the map."

"It isn't on the map. That's the problem. And don't presume I've a mind to turn you down. It's simply a matter of course to express my misgivings. Now what's your first task, Master? I am ever willing to serve."

Kayce nodded, undoubtedly charmed he'd won Jason over so easily. He scrambled back to his long table and hefted from it an iron cannonball approximately eight inches in diameter. Carefully adjusting his spectacles with the back of his hand, he asked Jason if he knew what it was. Jason admitted he didn't.

"Mid-nineteenth century. Predates the Civil War. Never used in combat, yet my extra-perception tells me there's something rather tragic about it."

"And you need me to catalogue it? Chart its power? Is that it?"

"Yes, my friend, but also to retrieve its story. You see, my last Eye quit after a month. The contract requires a certain degree of mental resiliency."

Kayce bent and rolled it with the loud, pendulous warbling of a gutter ball. Jason could have avoided it, but instead allowed the cannonball to pass into his auric field. His own precious spirit flowed from his feet, wrapping itself around it and lifting it from the floor. The projection—this one a dull, rusty red—launched from the ball on contact.

A fort of some sort. Men in stuffy army uniforms standing around a powder room, eating sandwiches, joking, laughing and killing time. One man in particular—older than the rest, with a bushy mustache and stripes on his sleeves—bent to check a charge near an outward-facing mortar. The fort seemed well-armed, with a dozen other cannons arrayed in a defensive posture along the masonry of its bulwark.

The fellow in stripes barked orders and then struck a match to light his hand-rolled cigarette, a simple bout of ill-timed bravado. Distracted by the loud behavior of his young subordinates, he mistakenly assumed the match was out. He tossed it near a pile of charges. They ignited, causing a rather loud explosion. Jason couldn't see how the man died or if this ball was directly involved, and the truth was he didn't want to. The experience sickened him, though it was comforting to acknowledge the man must not have suffered long.

Jason wrenched his tendrils of spiritual energy from the ball. He felt drained and vaguely nauseous, an odd sensation. He bent and began collecting extra energy from the ground, literally pulling it into himself, gathering it and leeching it from the room. Like a man dying of thirst, he drank it in, feeling rejuvenated though not entirely himself.

"Have you ever considered the danger of these things, Mr. Kayce?" he said.

John smiled. "Of course I have. I know my affairs better than you, young man."

"I'm older than you. That's something you should keep in mind."

"But of course. Perhaps I misperceived your true nature. Alarmingly young. It may be an asset tonight. You see, I've a deal to make under the auspices of a very unreliable actor. At least, that's how he's always presented himself. Do you know anything about wealthy and powerful men? The address is 144th street at Cicero. The time is seven o'clock. May I please see the Dead Man's Hand?"

"Yes, though it's a devilish trade you deal in, John," said Jason. "I don't doubt you'll have a great many things to work off in the afterlife."

Kayce's smile disappeared. "The Dead Man's Hand, please. We wouldn't want to be late."

* * * * *

The dead met with a dream-like fugue in the long form of spiritual transit. In truth, it was the only time a ghost could find rest. But as Jason journeyed from Kayce's leather tube to the Vanderbilt Casino, owned by one Mr. Wilhelm Blades, none of his dreams were restful. He saw his mother and father, his two sisters and their children. He'd not visited the family in some time. His parents would be very old by now, and his nieces and nephews might have families of their own.

As he tumbled through a white and golden slip space, and all worldly troubles subsided, he found he couldn't let go of the projection that had spilled from the cannonball. The more he considered it, the more foreign it seemed. He felt he heard the man in stripes speaking in his deep, gruff voice as his boys ate their sandwiches.

Look alive, men. No one'll douse you if you catch fire. This isn't the time nor place for horseplay!

And then only a moment later, strike of the match, flick of the wrist, and a shower of sparks and flames. Jason felt like probing the memory further. It occurred to him that in the projection, the poor, doomed man had held the match in his left hand, but here in his dream state, Jason perceived the match in his right. Strange. His own subconscious voice spoke to him, a common occurrence in the fugue. *You're not wrong. There are inconsistencies. Many more than you've deciphered.*

And why is that? Jason asked.

Listen, Jason, when you awaken you'll find yourself in a rather rude position. The bastards have waylaid your master. If he survives this next part, it'll be a miracle. They've already shot him, you see. The fugue has delayed you only a moment or two.

Shot him? What do you mean?

Look alive, soldier. Things get rough from here.

Jason exited the fugue. He found himself on the floor of a gaudy and noisy casino, chained to Kayce's ankle. Astral blue links, jangling and heavy. Kayce lay against the underside of an overturned casino table. He seemed bewildered and enraged to see Jason. A large blood stain covered the shoulder of his white dress shirt.

"Where have you been, Eye!" he shouted.

A gunshot rang out, the ricochet of a bullet pinging loudly against the table. The interior of the casino was an obnoxious red and gold. It appeared to be empty, no guests collecting tokens or losing their shirts. Nevertheless, electric signs, slot machines, gaming alarms and televisions blared. Jason imagined the red hot sulfuric smell of gunpowder in the air. Another shot rang out.

"What's going on," Jason asked. "Who's trying to murder you?" He rattled the chain, attempted to break it in his hands. It was made of stern stuff.

"Some kind of confinement spell," said Kayce. "Blades is a tough old fool, I'll give him that. Now tell me why you're late."

"He's late, Kayce, because he discovered your cannon shot is a forgery!" a loud voice called. "I can smell it on him. You'd have to be far shrewder than the preeminent dullard John Kayce to fool a man like me!"

Jason peered over the casino table. Near the entrance of the great red room, up a set of a dozen wide carpeted steps, sat a man in a wheelchair. He wore an old-fashioned white suit and was flanked on either side by a henchman. A silver handgun hung limply from his hand, the barrel dangling against his leg.

"I can see you, geist!" he said. "Don't think for a moment I can't. I need neither spectacles nor any other tricks. That man is a fraud, and if you find yourself chained to his rotten corpse for all eternity, it will be too soon!"

Land of the living be damned. Kayce grunted and dabbed at his shoulder with a quivering hand. "I admit it, Jason. I forged the ball. Somehow Wilhelm spotted it even when you couldn't. I had no idea."

"No idea of what?" Jason asked.

"That I am far more talented than some dead rep from a blasted agency pool!" called Blades. "Boys, go kill that scoundrel. Make sure I get my money's worth."

His two henchmen laughed. As they drew near,

one of them brandishing the cannonball in question, Jason discovered they weren't men at all, but rather, some kind of mechanized or wooden constructs. Each had a deep green rune imprinted on its forehead. Beneath white fedoras, curly locks of springy wire or perhaps oak or teak shavings bounced. Jason was an expert runesman. One rune read *George* and the other, *Gracie*.

Sporting teeth of sparkling ivory, George looked the more metallic of the two. In a deep baritone, he chuckled, "Let's go get him, Gracie. Say g'night for me."

"G'night, Gracie," said the second construct, his voice even deeper than George's.

"Listen, Jason," said Kayce, "I don't know how to get this across, but I was in the right and Wilhelm is wrong. I only reserve the forgeries for buyers I don't trust."

The two constructs rounded the casino table. Rather strange-looking up close. Pointed chins and off-centered features. One of Gracie's eyes was blue and the other brown, and two fingers on George's right hand—the same which clutched the cannonball—looked more like needling pincers.

George leaned over and got in Jason's face. Creatures such as these were not alive, more like automatons, though each rune did hold a spark of spiritual energy. Their creator, most likely Mr. Blades himself, would have had to gather and cage a large amount of spirit to animate them. Much magic would've been needed to perform such an operation, and magic's first law dictated each spell, hex, and charm had a physical price. Jason thought about Blades' ruined legs. Such would have been equal to the task, one leg for each chuckling henchman.

"Hey ghosty," George said, "you're just a patsy and we know it. Wrong place, wrong time. But it don't matter to us. You're with this joker, which means we gotta take it out of your hide."

Gracie snatched the ball from George's pincers, saying, "The boss had nice plans for this little beauty. Ain't that right, boss?"

"That's Mr. Blades to you," Wilhelm said. "And yes, I had plans for it. Do me a favor and get on with it, would you, boys?"

"Now you tell us something, mister," said George. "Why is it you think you can cheat the boss like that?"

Gracie snarled at John and in one brutal, gut-wrenching thrust, slammed the cannonball into his face. Blood and brains splattered the underside of the casino table. Rather than springing free as it should, Kayce's essence left his body in a spray of spirit that wrapped itself around the ball and consumed it in a blinding shower of ectoplasmic sparks.

* * * * *

Across the city, behind the locked doors of John's lab, spirits began to awaken. First just one or two, but as awareness of his demise spread, dozens emerged from their artifacts.

The instant John died, the fisherman who lived in the marlin, one Bart Finnegan, managed to break his terrible, tragic loop and stop himself just before he threw his fishing line too hard into the sea. He steadied himself, shifted his weight so as not to fall, and gazed out over the water.

"Two hundred years I been killing myself. And for what?" he uttered. Nearby, the group of children who'd been frolicking in the sun stopped their play and watched him. So the evil bastard was dead, which meant they were prisoners no longer.

Turning to them, he said, "Young uns. I do believe we are free."

The trio of children approached him slowly. The eldest, a girl Bart didn't know and had never met in life, nodded at the sea and said, "We tried to stop you, sir. Again and again, but it was always too late. That man ..."

"I know, girly. He was a bad feller, and it's up to us to put his rotten spirit in its place. You remember the incantation he always spoke? The one which kept us locked up tight?"

She said she did, and together they recited it. The spell broke in a hazy flash of light, and the four of them tumbled from the marlin onto the floor of Kayce's lab. Bart didn't recognize any of the other spirits who had begun to gather, nor could he easily reckon their numbers. They packed the room, and each and every one of them spat and swore, angry and horrified they'd been made to suffer so long.

"So the old git is dead!" shouted a woman dressed in royal finery. "Never thought I'd see the day. G'bye, Mr. Kayce. May you rot and make many an earthworm merry!"

A dark skinned young man, of eastern or African persuasion, uttered something in broken English.

"What did he say?" asked a sickly, grey-haired gentleman covered in his own vomit.

The young fellow spoke louder. "I say we torture man and he Eye. Marooned in scroll thousands year as carrion peck at I skull. Long line of such filthy dreg. He suffer this night."

"What say, chap?" asked Barton. "You'd like to torture the poor devil? Just for the fun of it? I may be a shell of the man I was, but my old mater would never forgive me."

"Agreed," said an old-world painter, garb and cap smeared with colorful oils. "I'm not too keen on revenge. Teaching the bastard a lesson, though, now that does sound rather appealing."

"Let's follow that damn Eye of his," Barton said. "His leather tube must be around here somewhere."

* * * * *

Jason stared in horror at the gory mess that had once been John Kayce. Imprisoned now inside the cannonball, presumably having supplanted the false projection that'd resided there, John would forever re-experience his own mortal terror. Upon the man's passing the spectral chain that had tied him to Jason remained sturdy and steadfast, only now Jason was permanently tethered to the cannonball itself.

"Ha! Never saw that coming, I'll bet!" shouted Blades.

No, Jason had not. George and Gracie trudged up the steps to Wilhelm's wheelchair and lifted him down to the casino floor. The old millionaire wheeled himself over so he could gawk at John's corpse.

"I barely knew him," Jason said. "I've only been employed by him a day."

"Yet here we are," said Blades. "Don't cut him loose, boys. Let him sit there and think about the company he keeps."

It occurred to Jason he could take refuge in the ball, an unsavory prospect if there ever was one. He reached into his pocket and withdrew the Dead Man's Hand.

"You see this?" he said. "This means my job isn't done. I'll have to remain with Kayce no matter what. The least you could do is cut me loose so I can inform my agency."

"Don't be simple," Blades said. "Let's go, boys. Nothing more to see here."

A blinding barrage of white and blue electrostatic discharge filled the casino. Slot machines spun up and spat coins, while chandelier lights flickered wildly. A great pressure seized the room, sucking Jason toward a spot somewhere behind Blades and his constructs.

Hundreds of ghosts blinked into existence. The variety was stunning, all periods and ages, men women and children, animals even, a few horses, a cow and several dogs. At their head, directly opposite Wilhelm Blades, stood the fisherman of the marlin, Bart. Next to him, a young man with deep mocha skin and three children—two boys and one girl—who looked rather terrified.

Wilhelm yelped. His constructs unholstered their weapons.

"Now what's this?" Gracie said. "Who the hell are you, ghosties?"

Bart the fisherman balked and declared. "We're the ones been wronged most by one Mr. John Kayce. Who the hell are you?"

"What this place? Is too loud," said the man with

mocha skin. He reached into the satchel at his waist and removed a rather familiar papyrus scroll, clutching it to his chest as if he needed its protection.

"Now I recognize you," Jason said. "You're that poor Egyptian fellow. The buzzards picked at your skull in that sand-swept nether realm."

"There ain't no such thing as nether realms, Eye. Just worlds of suffering without end," the fisherman said. "And if not for that man there—egad, look at the blood! They sure did a number on you, eh Johnny?"

Blades shrieked, "I was right! The artifacts are prisons! Oh how marvelous." He paused, sensing perhaps he'd made the wrong comment at the wrong time. "What I mean to say is, may I go now, kind and noble spirits? My constructs and I have important business to attend to."

The little girl of the marlin, taller and older than her two young companions, nudged Bart and motioned for him to bend down and lend an ear. He did so, and she cupped a hand over her mouth and whispered to him.

"Yes, young 'un. Which means he'll not escape our wrath any more than this Eye," Bart said. The fisherman twitched his ghostly fingers and formed a bright blue energetic ball in his hands. Spreading his palms wide, he fired it at Jason's chain. It snapped in half with a loud, echoing clang. An etheric chain link sprung free and pelted Mr. Blades in the forehead.

"Ouch!" he said, and jerked so the pocket of his jacket spilled its contents into his lap. A few bullets, falling heavily onto the floor. A pack of chewing gum, bubble flavored. And last but not least, a leather transit tube marked with a large black rune that read, *Belladonna Kayce*. Without thinking, Jason leapt for it and slipped into the fugue.

* * * * *

John's wife, Belladonna, had felt her husband's death as a deep, heartrending ache within her bosom. That bosom, ample though it was, wasn't one of flesh but of copper, gold, and steel. Belladonna Kayce was not human. She was a construct, and she'd been cheating on John for years. Parts of her body—the only parts that mattered to Wilhelm Blades—were made of a soft silicone resembling skin, but the rest of her was cold as an empty grave, and though some small piece of her loved Blades for his tenacity and sheer wicked intent, Belladonna felt true remorse and regret when it occurred to her John had passed.

"My goodness," she uttered, her voice sheer and tinny. She turned away from her winter lilies, bright and yellow though they were. Her garden house, a tall and narrow affair, hidden away on the back five acres of the Kayce family property, was secluded enough she rarely received visitors.

Mr. Kayce himself had secreted her away upon marrying her. Belladonna sat in a large wicker chair strong and sturdy enough to support her heavy, heaving frame. Another man had made her some twenty years before, losing his life in the process. In that time, she'd come to think of John as a surrogate creator. She spent the next several moments wishing she could cry, contemplating for the first time in her unnatural life the mysteries of a world that would barter such love and sever it wholly.

As she readied herself to phone the rest of John's family, an unexpected wind blew through the garden house. A single ghost, whom Belladonna recognized as John's newest Eye, popped into existence beside her potted cactus.

"Who are you?" he asked. "And why are you in Blades' pocket?"

Reflexively, misunderstanding the implication, she said, "His pocket? Why I never!"

Wilhelm Blades was no ordinary man. He'd mastered the art of astral projection and had made love to Belladonna in spirit more times than she could count. John dead now, his new Eye scrambling to get away. It meant Wilhelm would arrive soon, for he'd not give her up now he had no competition.

"You're a construct," said the Eye.

"So I am. Were you there when he died?"

"I was. Blades killed him. Why are you in his pocket? Mr. Kayce never would have—"

"Oh, I see, his pocket! You mean the transit tube," said Belladonna. "Where is John's spirit, young man? Why have you come instead of him?"

"He's imprisoned in that damned artifact of his. And I need to get the hell out of here before Blades and that ghastly horde come to do the same to me."

He turned to flee, but Belladonna closed her eyes, concentrated her will, and with her spectral energy flung a green energetic hand out at Jason, gripping him by the shoulder and holding him in place.

"You aren't going anywhere, Eye. If Wilhelm will have words with you—"

Another spirit popped into the garden house. He was tall and muscular, with a lean, powerful frame and a menacing glint in his eye.

Wilhelm had arrived.

For decades on end, he'd neglected his body to become a spiritual dynamo. He wore a toga and sported a beard, and nestled in the middle of his forehead was an indigo sphere that beamed and pulsed. Belladonna both admired and loathed him. He had taken and she had given, catching his eye one night as he spied on her husband from afar.

My love, your husband has expired, said Blades.

"I know."

"And you don't seem too damn sad about it." Jason said.

Belladonna scoffed. "Don't you dare lump me in with Wilhelm. I loved that man."

Unfortunately my dear, it's a moot point. I plan to destroy this infernal cannonball and end John's unnatural life for good. Blades gestured and swung his arms around, and lo and behold, the cannonball appeared before him. Belladonna's mechanical jaw dropped. Transportation of physical energy. Wilhelm was far more formidable than John had anticipated.

"That's impossible. How'd you do that?" asked Jason.

Mind over matter, my ghastly friend.

"How are you going to kill him? Spirit cannon be unmade, just as it cannot be made. You've amassed too much power, Blades."

Wilhelm grinned. Cocking an eyebrow, he flicked his wrists and forced the cannonball to orbit him. *You've no idea what I'm capable of, geist. I intend to kill every last spirit entangled in this loathsome affair. Now stand still.*

He flung the ball at Jason. It passed through him, dragging his essence with it until he spiraled, flailed and disappeared within it.

Nothing will keep us from each other now, my dear, Wilhelm said.

* * * * *

Jason once again found himself on the casino floor, surrounded by the multitude of ghosts, chained to Kayce's ankle, though for the time being, John looked safe, and in manner of speaking, alive. He argued with his former prisoners while the static image of Gracie held aloft the ball, frozen in place mere inches from his head.

"Look, the Eye has graced us with his presence at last," a woman in distinct royal clothing declared. "Neat trick running away like that, young turk, but I'm afraid you're no better for it."

"I'm not young, and I know exactly what I'm doing," Jason replied.

"Jason, have you seen my wife?" said Kayce. "Does she grieve for me? How does she look?"

"Artificial, though I would expect nothing less from you," Jason said.

"Trust me, young master, Johnny done more unnatural things than you can shake a stick at," Bart the fisherman said. "Nothing can be done about it any of it now, though."

"Not so," Jason said. He extended a hand to the young Egyptian, who fairly cowered beside Bart, his face dour and beleaguered. "Sir, if you'll permit me."

The young fellow hastily stuffed the papyrus scroll into the satchel at his waist. "Do not permit. Do not."

"I can do nothing to help our situation unless all of you are willing to cooperate. That scroll is a destruction hex, if I'm not too terribly mistaken. Normally, I shouldn't think it would work, but seeing as Blades is in his energetic form for the time being …"

"He is?" asked Kayce. "What's the bastard doing?"

"You don't want to know. I mean that, John," Jason said. "You're the only one who has to stay in this place. There's a backdoor for the rest of us, and I don't think Whilhelm has realized it yet. Master, I assume you know what you have to do?"

John Kayce frowned and winced. "Yes, I suppose I do."

Jason clapped him on the back and in one swift motion, jerked Gracie's static arm so that the ball reconnected with his face. Blood and brains splattered the underside of the casino table and hundreds of ghosts leapt from the artifact to fill the rather narrow interior of Mrs. Kayce's garden house. She and Blades made love on the floor behind a row of fruit and vegetables, cucumbers and melons. Before he knew what hit him, Jason, the fisherman, and the young Egyptian were on top of him.

"Now what's this!" he shouted.

"This, Mr. Blades, is the termination of your essence. And not soon enough, if you ask us," Bart said. "Boy, hit him with the scroll!"

His voice rough and reluctant, the Egyptian read from the papyrus, pronouncing a flowing set of verses that had an immediate and substantial effect. A slit formed at the top of Wilhelm's head, right above the spot his indigo spectral eye glinted.

Blades shrieked. A sound like a freight train filled the garden house, the nude Mrs. Kayce scrambling to get away. In a shower of sparks, Blades' spectral essence disbanded and flooded the floor in a quivering puddle of ectoplasm, there to wiggle and jiggle without determined form. Jason asked Mrs. Blades if she was all right.

"Of course I'm not all right! Now please take me to my husband. And hand me that night dress. Naked as the day I was made!"

Jason sighed. He bent over, touched the cannonball and produced the projection of Mr. Kayce. His wife would have to grieve his passing until some manner of escape could be formulated.

"You men and women, children and animals, you may go wherever you wish, provided you don't interfere in the affairs of the living," Jason said. "I'm heading back to my agency to ask for a leave. I've had quite enough excitement to last the rest of my afterlife."

"You aren't serious, lad," Bart Finnegan said. "We

need your help. How're we supposed to get along now that we're free?"

Jason frowned at him, for the first time in ages desperate to be near his family.

"I really don't care, Bart," he said. "I'm long overdue, and now that I recognize it, I've got no reason to be anywhere but home. Now get out of my way. It's a long way to Massachusetts, and no damned Dead Man's Hand will stop me ever again."

"Blue danced with yellow, then.
Spinning and twisting
and sparking
against each other...."

BLUE DANCING WITH YELLOW

Originally Appeared in Stupefying Stories: Showcase, September 2016

MY dearest Angelica,

Pen and paper are all I have left. The sky split in half six weeks ago, and since it did, New York has been in the dark. No electronic devices, no electricity of any kind.

Do they have thunder beings in Boston? Do they stomp around your mother's street? I guess I already know the answer, but still I feel compelled to ask. Do they have never-ending hurricanes? Do they have the dance?

You'll never read this letter. I'll write it out, and then I'll cry over it with a bottle of looted Bacardi, and then stuff it in my sock drawer with the others. You always asked me to tell you the wildest stories when you were little. Here's one for you. Here's one the entire world wasn't ready for.

September sixteenth, 2:29 in the morning. That was the instant the clocks stopped. I was lying down to sleep. Tired, spent, long day at the office. I reached over to flick off the light and ...

The lights went out. Not just for me. For everyone everywhere in the city. The sky opened up—a deep, crashing roll and rumble—and then the hurricane winds came smashing against my windows. A bolt of lightning hurled itself downward, charred the air, slammed headlong into Central Park. It flattened trees, lit them on fire. It left a crater the size of a house.

The bolt rebounded from the impact, leapt skyward. It popped and frayed, grew arms, legs, a head, and it pirouetted in the sky, and did a summersault, and then the bolt of lightning, it spoke to the city.

"New York!" it called, voice of crackling static, lit tongue of snapping voltage. "Hear me now, New York City!"

And New York listened. How could we not? The voice played across smartphones and televisions and laptops and even the little wall speakers people use to buzz apartment dwellers.

This being of light, this being of thunder, it slammed back to Earth. It took hold of its mighty chest, and it pulled away electric skin, and laughed and chortled from the pain. It threw out its arms, and skin flew away, shook out its legs, and its skeleton was bare. I swear to you, dearest Angelica. Its electric skeleton threw fingers of light, slinking juice writhing from rib to rib, wrapping round radius bones, slipping over and through the jaw, to the skull, to two wretched, wreathed eyes of deepest, startling blue.

"New York City!" it said. "I'm here to dance with my lady! You may call us gods. You may! You may worship us in whatever way seems best. But tonight we dance!"

And as the thunder being spoke this final word, *dance*, a second bolt of lightning reached down from the heavens and slammed against Central Park's Great Lawn and lit an acre of grass on fire. It spread itself out, yellow, taut tendrils twirling. It drew up, grew limbs, grew hips, grew great bouncing breasts. It spotted the blue skeleton thunder being, and then it giggled, deep and rumbling, brassie enough to rattle my windows.

Blue danced with yellow, then. Spinning and twisting and sparking against each other. Wild, exploding, ebullient fireworks. The vivid, delirious colors of a fever dream. He threw her high, and her crackling dress flashed and gleamed. The rain came down by the bucketful. Streets were awash from Harlem to Midtown. Flooding subways, burst retaining walls, power stations exploding in the night.

When they were finished, when the thunder beings had danced their dance, their chests heaved with electric exhaustion. Blue lay yellow on her back, gently, right there atop the *Imagine* emblem of Lennon's Strawberry Fields, and he kissed her softly on the lips, and then he slid himself between her thighs and he ...

You know something, Angelica, my dear? Even though you'll never read this, you're still too young to know the details. Suffice it to say, very soon the thunder beings slept there beneath the hurricane rains, silent, still, and content.

As morning approached, I and a few dozen others in my building ventured outside, parkas wrapped tightly around our bodies, never letting eighty-mile-an-hour gusts knock us off our feet. We made it down to Central Park, to a crowd of thousands. We vied for spots to watch them sleep, these thunder beings, these gods of light. Blue was the first to awaken. He yawned and melted the sidewalk with his breath. The crowd cried out. He simply chuckled and sat up. I tell you, he was twelve stories tall if he was a foot. Finger bones wrapped placidly around a smoldering tree trunk.

"Wake up, my dear," he cooed, "the little ones are watching us."

Lady yellow awoke, and she batted her eyelashes. Her flickering cheeks reddened at the sight of us.

"You know?" said blue. "I think we like it here. I want another dance. I want to make love a thousand more times here in this city."

And he said he would, and each night for six weeks, that's exactly what he's done.

Hmph.

Yeah.

It's funny, isn't it? The stories we tell ourselves? I guess I'm just trying to relive better days. Oh they're not lies, Angelica. Not really. What would you rather I say? There's no such thing as thunder beings? Humanity has truly mucked things up? Super storms every week now? New York City and the entire Eastern Sea Board decimated?

No, I like skeleton blue and lady yellow better. And I like the idea you're still out there, with your mother, safe from all this mayhem and death. I love you, my dearest Angelica. I always have. I always will.

Every day the same, every day the same. Even now I can hear them. Doing the Two-Step down in Central Park. I can hear blue dancing with yellow.

I learned a lot of things in Tumbleweed Army.
I learned how to march,
how to roll up into a little ball to protect myself.
Learned how to say, "Yes, ma'am!" like I meant it.

TUMBLEWEEDS AND LITTLE GIRLS

Originally appeared on PodCastle.org, March 2016

THEY had the tumbleweed ambassador on the news a month before the big battle. The news guy and news girl said he was intelligent, and then a local representative of the Plains and Wildlife Service translated for him because tumbleweeds can't talk and must sign everything by rolling and hopping and what not.

"We mean your people no harm," said the Plains and Wildlife Service guy. He spoke kind of slow and choppy. I guessed he wasn't actually, what do you call it? Fluent in tumbleweed?

He said, "The war has started, whether you realize it or not. The Prairie Queen has an army of deer, antelope and coyotes. She's got the power of fire. She murdered our Wizard Father and made her castle from our dead tumbleweed brothers and sisters. The crazy bitch!"

I winced at this last word. I'm only twelve years old, after all. My dad used to talk real rough like that. He used to cuss and laugh and say to me, "Don't repeat that to your mother, Amie Masterson. I don't want to fight no little girl." Then we'd roughhouse a bit. My dad died last year, though. Some kind of cancer. Mom never told me which.

I don't usually watch the late news. I'm supposed to be in bed. But Mom passed out on the sofa early. I laid a blanket over her and picked the empty wine bottle off its side so it wouldn't drip on the carpet.

The Plains and Wildlife Service guy said, "Have you not noticed her spot-fires outside your city? We want to kill your precious girls!"

The tumbleweed popped up into the air and spun angrily.

Plains and Wildlife Guy said, "Oh, I'm sorry, I'm sorry. We want to *utilize* your precious girls. We have no defenses. We need soldiers. The Prairie Queen cannot stand against the wealth of your girls. Or so we believe."

There was some more talking. I was getting sleepy.

The news guy said, "And of course we know the city has been expanding into the Queen's prairieland at an exponential rate."

And the news girl said, "Right you are, Tom. In retrospect, that may have been a huge mistake. Oops."

And then a commercial for local heating and cooling repair came on. I went to kiss Mom on the forehead. She moaned softly, smiled for a second, and then settled into a noisy, listless snore. Mom is a good mother, but I think Dad dying did some stuff to her. I guess that's normal. She never used to drink wine.

There was a knock at the door. I was scared for a second, but only because Mom said never to open the door to strangers at such a late hour.

There was another knock.

"Mom," I said, "someone at the door."

Mom didn't wake up. I nudged her, shook her, but still nothing, all snores, drool dribbling from the corner of her mouth. I went to the door, looked through the peephole.

There was nobody there.

"The heck?" I said. I slid back the deadbolt and opened the door.

A tumbleweed sat on our welcome mat. It had a leather glove duct-taped to its scrawny, scratchy limbs. It was kind of a big tumbleweed. The color of autumn wild grass. It leaned in to, like, look in our house.

"Is this because I'm a precious girl?" I said.

The tumbleweed shook.

"And you're recruiting all the girls and that means me, right?"

It shook again.

"Only thing is I can't leave. Mom'll be super pissed. Oops. Mom'll be super angry."

The tumbleweed rolled, over and over, until the glove and duct tape came undone and stuck and sat limp and kind of sad on our porch. The tumbleweed wiggled and bent toward the glove.

I shrugged and picked it up. There was a big rock inside. There was also some red dirt. I brought the dirt to my nose to sniff it. It smelled salty, briny, kind of like how I imagine the ocean smells, like vast rotting shipwrecks beneath the waves where porpoises and turtles swim and play.

"What's this stuff?" I said.

The tumbleweed smashed into my leg. My hand jerked, the dirt flew, a bunch of it went up my nose.

I sneezed.

Someone said, *Me entiendes?*

I sneezed again. A big cloud of red flew from my nostrils.

Someone said, *Ne me comprenez-vous?*

"Huh?" I snorted. "S'that even English?"

Oh, English, English! Oh, of course! Yes, how sally of me.

"What? Sally?" I wriggled my nose and wiped allergy tears from my eyes.

Silly! Silly! Of course! Stupid Dumb-Dust. I'm dumb, you know? All tumbleweeds are dumb. Call me Aaron. Aaron Sisymbrium Altissimum. Don't worry about that last part. That's my family name. Are you ready to be a soldier, girl?

"Soldier?" I said. "You mean to fight the Prairie Queen?"

That's precisely what I mean. Time is short. Matters are barbiturate.

"Barbiturate?"

Aaron twitched. *Desperate! Desperate! If we don't stop her now, she'll kill all the tumbleweeds, and then, girl, she'll kill all the humans, too.*

I looked over my shoulder. Mom was still snoring away on the couch. Wine makes adults snore. That's something I learned.

Come on, soldier, said Aaron, *no more dilly dallying. Don't you want to make your fellow humans proud?*

* * * * *

I learned a lot of things in Tumbleweed Army. I learned how to march, how to roll up into a little ball to protect myself. Learned how to say, "Yes, ma'am!" like I meant it. Most of all, I learned coyotes and deer and antelope were really scary because they could eat the tumbleweeds and break the wizard's spell and use their shoulder-mounted flamethrowers to burn everything. The Prairie Queen had the power of fire. She wanted to burn it all, burn the world, which I guess included my home and my mom, which is why I stayed.

There was a girl there called Jade. She was an older girl. Really pretty, with deep almond skin and bright green eyes. We'd be in the middle of flamethrower-dodging exercises, and she'd come up to me and look at the way I was darting and dodging around, and she'd say, "Looking real good, Masterson. Looking real sharp."

The tumbleweeds didn't do any of the teaching or drilling themselves. They only knew tumbling. They left it to all the thirteen and fourteen-year-olds to teach us everything we needed to know. Maybe they should have asked for the real army, the adult army. Even they seemed weirded out by a little girl army, and sometimes they acted like they didn't know how they'd ended up with us at all.

If the adult army was looking for us, they never found us, secret and hidden away on the outskirts of the city like we were. Also the tumbleweeds had this special concealing magic. The last thing they had left of their Wizard Father.

Aaron told me, *Our Wizard Father was a great man. He granted us intelligence and the freedom we so cherish. But the concealing magic's fading. We can't stay hidden from the Queen forever.*

I was like, okay, you're fine, the older girls know everything. They've designed this whole thing and know everything there is to know. That's probably why our uniforms were pink and sparkly, and why our flags carried pictures of Justin Bieber and Lady Gaga, and why even though the cutoff age was fourteen, you could tell they were serious and skilled and were girls on a mission, girls ready to kill.

I missed my mom. I'm not going to lie about that. I missed her so bad it didn't matter to me she didn't listen anymore when I talked to her about school, or that I always saw her crying first thing in the morning, or that everything Dad made her promise when he was in the hospital sort of, well, just went forgotten and we didn't talk about it. I was in that army for four weeks, then we had the big battle, but I never forgot Mom, and I guess she never forgot me, but I couldn't say goodbye to her just in case I might die, because the tumbleweeds were real, real strict about enemy code breakers and antelope misinformation squads.

* * * * *

One night as I was laying down to sleep in my tent, Jade came and undid the tent flap and she and a few girls brought in a little white cupcake with a single candle flickering and hopping kind of like a tumbleweed.

"What's this?" I said sleepily.

"It's your birthday, Masterson," said Jade.

"My birthday?"

She nodded and said, "Make a wish."

I wished to kiss a boy, but knew it probably wouldn't come true because there were no boys for miles and miles. Me and the girls shared the cupcake, but the cupcake was made out of mashed potatoes, because the tumbleweed galley only had potatoes because Aaron told us all you eat is potatoes in the army and we didn't argue.

"Jade," I said, choking down my last bite. "Do you think things will go back to normal after this? I mean, after we kill the Prairie Queen and all? Do you think all us girls can go back to how we were?"

Jade thought about this. She nodded. "Yes, I think we can. At least I hope we can. Wizards and Queens and Dumb-Dust, all that stuff shouldn't exist. I think it only exists because the world needs stuff to make you wonder. You know what I mean? My Dad always says, 'Boy it really makes you wonder'. I think that sort of thing is really important."

"Why?" I said.

One of the other girls chimed in. "Because

everything would be so boring otherwise."

"Boring's not bad," said Jade. "Boring's only bad if you get used to it. There's always people stepping on other people. Trying to take things that don't belong to them, you know? Because people get used to that, too. Like that spot where our city and their world meet up...."

* * * * *

So there was this spot where our city and their world met up. For miles and miles, our buildings rose high, and interstates ran, and traffic lights blinked red, yellow, green, red, yellow, green.

But on this spot, there were a few loose suburban fingers of little houses that looked nice but that also all looked the same, and those fingers kind of stretched out, and then they ended, and their world was beyond, the prairie world, high grass and rolling hills, pretty wildflowers and peaceful vistas.

The wind could rustle through, and it could carry a dry, dusty scent, and maybe there'd be pollen on the wind, but there were no honking car horns or televisions blaring. People didn't shout at each other. There were no people. The city wasn't there yet. Maybe it would be someday. Of course it would be. The city just kept growing and growing and growing, and nobody bothered to ask the Queen if it was okay. Nobody stopped to think it might be a bad thing if the prairie world got swallowed up, got paved over, with houses and restaurants and, you know, post offices and stuff built all over it.

We had the battle on that spot. It was time. No more hiding. Me and all the girls—thousands of girls—we lined up at the fence line of that last wandering suburban finger. The hot mid-afternoon sun beat down on us. Smell in the air like columbines. We came in our pink sparkly uniforms, with our flags waving. The grenade girls all had purple caps. Girls with rifles had big red badges on their chests. There were also film-crew girls, who'd appointed themselves to the rank, who held up smartphones and snapped selfies with the battlefield-to-be in the background.

I was light infantry, just like Jade, and that meant we had no weapons, only pig-tails and three-ring binders, because the tumbleweeds had chosen girls for a reason, and we all figured we'd be even scarier all dressed up for school.

Prairie Queen's afraid of school girls. Prairie Queen's afraid of school girls.

We kind of told each other that over and over again, sort of like a, what do you call it? A mantra?

Prairie Queen's afraid of school girls.

Prairie Queen's afraid of school girls.

And we said it again and again, and it made us less afraid, even though we knew we might die that day.

The ground beneath our feet trembled. Far off across the field, over the rise and fall of grassy hills, we saw the first ranks of animals and their flamethrowers. The coyotes were the fastest and lightest, and they ran ahead of the herd, belching fire, scorching earth, I guess to scare us. They howled and yipped at the antelope and deer. You kind of figure antelope and deer don't make noises, but they do. This strained, desperate, sharp kind of screaming noise. And when there are thousands of them—and there were thousands—it comes off like a banshee wail, like a great roaring throat sound loud as jet engines.

I don't know why, but the sound made us cry. It was so loud. The screaming, the yipping, the flames and flames and flames. I cried like I knew a soldier should never cry. But it was okay, because Jade cried, too. Maybe I felt like running home to my mom, and maybe Jade did also, but she didn't, she stood there like she was the bravest crying girl in the world, and she called back to us through her tears, "Steady, now! Wait until you see the whites of their eyes!"

And I didn't know what that meant, because animals don't have white eyes, but I stood my ground all the same, even though my legs trembled, even though the tears drenched my uniform and my tongue felt stuck to the roof of my mouth.

The tumbleweed commanders came rolling out to marshal our forces. I saw Aaron there with Commander Johnston Salsola Kali.

Commander Johnston waved a scraggly little twig-limb and said through the Dumb-Dust, *Today you do your species proud! Today you are not girls, but women! Human women of distinction, finery, and absolute quality. We have no idea how it is you came to defend us, but be not afraid, dear human beings! For though you may die—yes, you may die, yes, yes!—for though that may be so, remember, one and all, that the Queen may take your lives, but she shall never take your Sweden!*

In unison, the thousands-girl army said, "Huh?"

Commander Johnston said, *Bother! Freedom! Freedom! Freeeeeeedom!*

The army roared. Girls fired rifles in the air. They said, "Freeeeeeedom!" Even though freedom wasn't really the thing, but getting trampled and burned up, but a cry of freedom was enough, and I said it, too.

Jade told us to stand at the ready. We did. She told us to march ahead at the quick step. We did that, too. I think the older girls had watched old war movies before the battle, so everything they were telling us to do was really smart and accurate for what soldiers are supposed to do in battle.

We marched at the quick step. The rifle girls and grenade girls were right behind us. The rifle girls fired rounds over our heads. This was smart because the animals kind of flinched and froze at the noise.

Bang! Bang! Bang, bang, bang!

And anyway, it wasn't the animals we were after, but the Queen, who, tumbleweed intelligence told us, would be in the middle of her formations, in the mobile command station made of dead tumbleweed bodies all stuck together.

"Double-time, march!" said Jade.

We picked up the pace.

Coyotes snapped and howled at us. The deer and the antelope shot steady burning jets of fire. We began our dodging maneuvers, still in ranks, still in line, but dodging that fire like crazy.

A girl beside me—Kirsten—went down screaming. Our standard bearer went up in flames, but the next girl in line—a film-crew girl—picked up the smoldering flag and soldiered on, still bravely snapping selfies and snagging footage of the whole bloody mess.

And it occurred to me that the world was a crazy place. It made you wonder. Really made you wonder, you know? Girls weren't supposed to be soldiers. Were they? Were girls supposed to be soldiers? I bent over Kirsten. Girls weren't supposed to be soldiers, were they? Little girls? Kids and teenagers? I froze to the spot. I tried to touch her. Girls weren't supposed to be soldiers. She was too hot, too bubbling, too much melted Kirsten. Girls weren't supposed to be soldiers. They weren't, were—

Jade slapped me.

"Snap out of it, Masterson!" she said. "The command station! Look, it's right there!"

And it was right there. It looked like a castle on wheels. Made of tumbleweeds. Thousands upon thousands of poor dead tumbleweeds.

Burn the world! Burn it all!

Nobody else would die! Nobody!

Jade and I and the remnants of our unit—all told, seven girls—we darted in and out of flames and animals. Grenades exploded all around us. Dying things, dying from bullet wounds, dying from the burn.

We mounted the ramp of that mobile command station. We tried to punch through the tumbleweed walls, but the Queen had cast a spell, and the walls were solid as steel.

Jade told us to begin the chant, the mantra. We began it.

"Prairie Queen's afraid of school girls! Prairie Queen's afraid of school girls! Prairie Queen's afraid of school girls!"

The mobile command station rolled to a stop.

"Prairie Queen's afraid! Prairie Queen's afraid!"

The animals stopped. Their roaring streams and jets and flames. They stopped their screaming. The coyotes stopped howling and yipping and yapping.

"Prairie Queen's afraid of school girls!"

And our army stopped, too. Nobody told them what to do if the animals quit fighting. Nobody expected that. The battlefield went silent, all but the wind, and the flickering and popping of little grass fires here and there, and us seven girls, and our chanting, our mantra.

"Prairie Queen's afraid of school girls! Prairie Queen's afraid—"

"The Prairie Queen fears nothing!"

The voice boomed and echoed across the field. It was low, brassy, not human at all.

The command station exploded.

I went flying. I hit the ground. The air rushed from my lungs.

Tumbleweed shrapnel bit at me, scratched me up. I felt the pain of it, but I couldn't breathe, couldn't breathe at all.

The voice came again. With a kind of wispy whipcrack to each syllable.

"The Prairie Queen fears nothing! Nothing!"

Like the blast of a shotgun, my breath came back to me. I sucked in air like it was a thick milkshake, like the best chocolate milkshake I'd ever tasted.

Hands took hold of me, lifted me, jerked me up. My feet didn't touch the ground.

"You, girl! Do you think I fear you?"

It wasn't hands that had a hold of me. And it wasn't a nasty old Queen hovering inches from my face. I expected a scary old lady. The Prairie Queen was a blade of wild grass. Just a single, tall, stout blade of wild grass, with no face, no mouth, no eyes. Split from her body, willowy grass arms, with little willowy grass hands. She shook me. She said, "What stupidity! What inane musings! To think I could fear this dull creature! This girl. You people. You take so much. I will take from you!"

And then she threw me to the ground and started whipping me with her green grassy hands.

It stung. It slivered and sliced. I started bleeding. The girls just watched. The animals watched. Stunned.

"Help!" I said. "Help!"

"You will not take from me," screeched the Queen. "You will not take from me."

She whipped me. Welts and cuts and lacerations and ripping, tearing skin. I curled into a ball, like the older girls had taught us, but the whipping kept coming and kept coming and kept coming.

A little ball of fire started circling her wild grass head. The Queen said, "Burn the wizard. Burn the weeds. Burn your city to the ground!"

The ball grew and grew, and it circled faster and faster and—

Movement in the field.

A tumbleweed rolled and hopped over me and smashed into the Queen. The ball of fire circling her head exploded. The tumbleweed ignited. The Queen ignited, too.

"Masterson!" Jade was moving now. She tossed me a grenade. I pulled the pin and flicked it at the Queen.

The burning tumbleweed was in the way. I rolled behind an antelope carcass.

* * * * *

Mom found me bleeding on the sofa the next morning. There was a collection of wine bottles in our living room. And also a bunch of notebooks and pens and candy wrappers. And also pizza boxes because adults like whole pizzas and whole bottles of wine. That's something I learned.

Mom was drinking from a fresh bottle, sort of stumbling down the hall. She spotted me and said, "Oh my God, Amie?"

"Hi, Mom."

She dropped the bottle. Wine splashed our white carpet. She flung herself at me and started kissing me all over and crushing me.

"Ow!" I said. "Ow, Mom! I'm hurt. I'm bleeding."

"Jesus Christ, you're bleeding!"

"I know."

"Band-Aids! Hydrogen Peroxide!"

Mom patched me up as best she could. We both agreed I should go to the hospital, though. War's like that I guess. Sometimes people die. Sometimes they have to go to the hospital.

I watched the television as she fawned over me and poured peroxide over all my wounds. It bubbled and itched and burned. I still watched TV.

The Plains and Wildlife Service guy translated for Tumbleweed Commander Johnston. I didn't need him to, though.

Commander Johnston said, *This day, this VQ day, this victory over the Queen, we shall remember it always, just as we shall remember and honor anew a bond of brotherhood between weed kind and humankind. Let it never be said your people backed down when all free folk everywhere fell under the flaming, fiery yoke of prairie oppression.*

"It's absolutely crazy," said my mom. "It's crazy you girls had to do this."

Commander Johnston said, *Your girls are our heroes. We don't know why you sent them to us. All we know is we're glad you did.*

At this, Plains and Wildlife Guy paused, and, loud enough for the studio microphones to pick him up, he said, "What do you mean? You specifically said girls. Precious girls. You took them from us before we even—"

Commander Johnston quivered. *No, the girls were your idea. You're the ones who kept saying* girls, girls. *We asked for* pearls. *Thousands of precious* pearls. *As a means of currency. You know, to buy the aid of Southeast Asian mercenaries.*

Plains and Wildlife Service Guy looked into the camera. He shook his head. He sighed and rubbed his temples.

Regardless, said Commander Johnston, *it was the bravery of two—one weed, one girl—who gave us our victory, who stopped the wicked Queen and her lust for death and destruction. Aaron Sisymbrium Altissimum. Amie Masterson.*

My mom paused.

We owe our lives to you.

And then they showed the moment. The moment I don't think I'll ever forget. Aaron went rolling and hopping. It was Aaron. It was his death all over again. He smashed into the Queen. They both ignited. Jade threw me the grenade. I flicked it, rolled away. The screen went white for a moment. Big boom. And that was the end of the war.

"Dear God, Amie." My mom's voice was soft, barely above a whisper. "You did that?"

I nodded, staring at the screen, watching the replay, feeling all those grassy whip lashes again and again, feeling that impact, the way it hit the antelope carcass. Smell of gunpowder. Shrapnel in my leg. Antelope meat in my hair and in my mouth.

"You did that?" my mom said again.

"I did. I did do that."

"But you're just a little girl."

I put my hand on hers. Squeezed it.

"Mom?" I said.

"Yeah?"

"Too many wine bottles. Less wine, okay Mom?"

Mom hesitated. She nodded and said, "Okay, less wine."

"And Mom?"

"Yes, honey?"

"It was my birthday last week."

"I know."

"Can I have a cake? A real cake? Not a potato cake."

"What's a potato cake?"

"It's what you eat on your birthday when you're in the army. Don't you know anything about the army?"

Mom stared at me. She glanced at the TV, the footage, the whipping, the fire, the explosion. She shook her head.

"No," she said, "I guess I haven't the slightest clue."

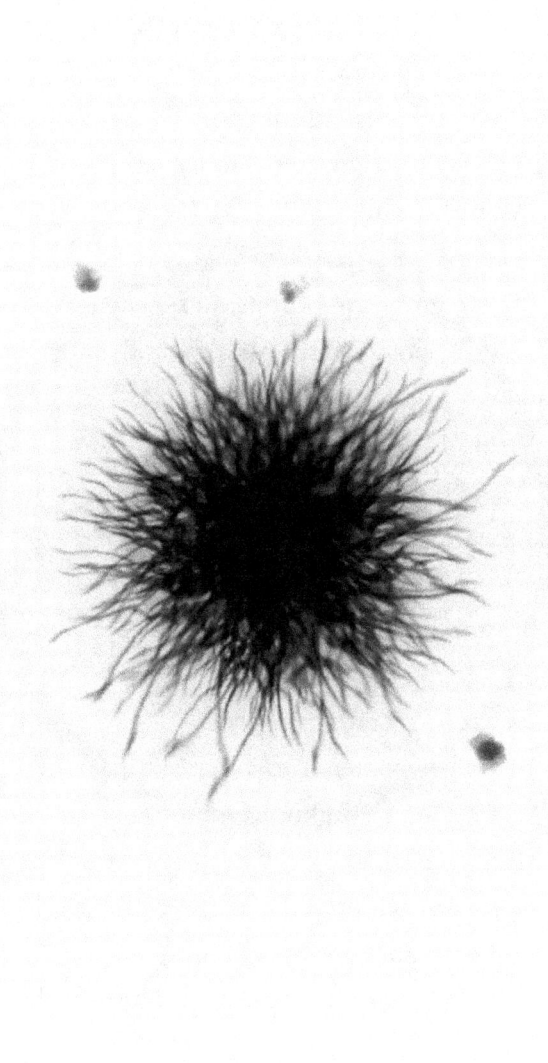

"Sometimes
I miss what it used to be like.
You know, being by
myself."

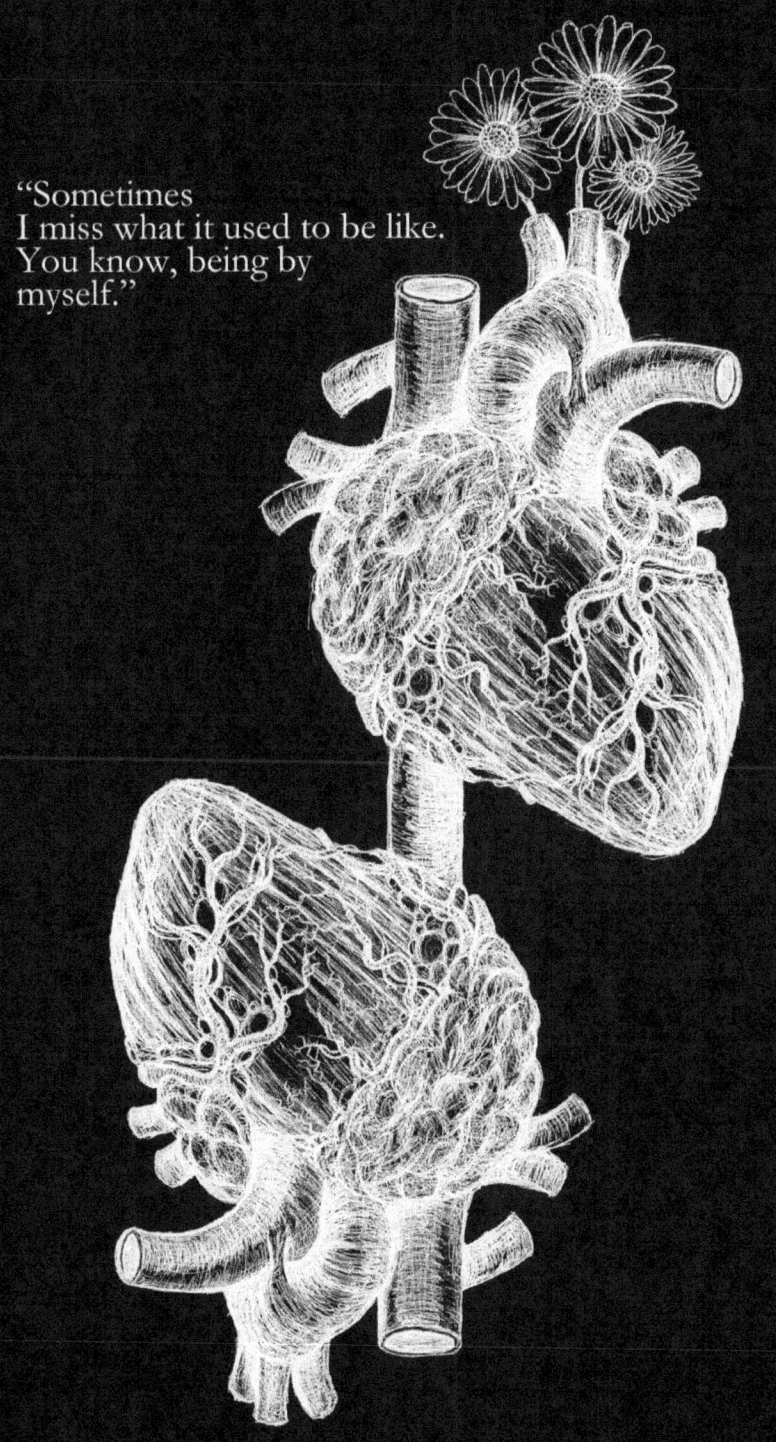

FOUR HEADS,
TWO HEARTS

ALEC'S heart leapt when he first laid eyes on Chelsea. Rather than finding her appearance alarming or freakish, he became lost in her eyes, the gorgeous green pair on the face to the left. She hit her tennis ball too hard and it spun and popped over the fence of the city park's tennis court, hopping along the grass and rolling to a stop at Alec's feet.

Before he could decide whether or not to pick it up, she called to him. "Hey, superstar, want to toss us that ball?"

Her second head, sitting there atop her right shoulder like a nested owl, snorted and exclaimed, "While we're young, superstar!"

He was on his lunch break. Sack sandwich in the park on a green park bench, while pigeons pecked and the sun stabbed sweltering mid-August rays. The color of the girl's hair reminded him of licorice. He swallowed his bite of baloney and cheese, picked up the ball and walked it to the fence. As he tossed it in, she said, "Hey, don't I know you? You're that guy who works IT two floors up, right?"

The second head snorted again. "Please, Chelsea dear, don't flirt. We're in the middle of a game, and we are winning."

Chelsea scowled. "Denise, we talked about this. You respect my privacy, and I'll respect yours."

"I think I'd remember seeing you," said Alec.

She grinned at him. "Yeah, understatement, huh? Only I just started last week."

"He's staring at you, dear," intoned the old lady. "And his mouth's hung wide open. Maybe we should charge him a dime so he can get the full circus experience."

"Charge me a dime?" said Alec. "No, wait, look at this."

Alec rolled up his sleeve.

There, attached to his forearm, sat a little two-inch head Alec had long since taken to calling Albert. Albert was a sappy old cuss who hated Mondays and liked to say rude things whenever politicians were on the television. He squinted in the sunlight, and in his small, gruff voice, shouted, "Holy sciatica, it's bright out here! It's bright!"

Chelsea stared at Albert. Albert stared back. Alec smiled pleasantly at Denise, and in turn, she glared at him long and mean enough he had to look away.

"Would you like to have lunch with me?" Alec asked.

Chelsea smiled. "Weren't you just eating a sandwich?"

"Forget it, I'm still hungry. I'd like to have lunch with you. Does that sound cool?"

Chelsea laughed and said it did.

* * * * *

Alec was not born with Albert. As far as the doctors could tell, Albert was a benign tumor that, for no known medical reason, started swearing and demanding scotch one Tuesday afternoon. Similarly, Chelsea was not born with Denise. It was a head transplant, a life-saving medical experiment. Chelsea had recently lost her mother, and at the time she'd been heartbroken. She gained a lifelong companion and saved a dying woman in a single twenty-hour surgery.

"Sometimes I miss what it used to be like. You know, being by myself," Alec told her as they walked along the business fronts on Fourth. They'd elected to go the three long blocks from the park to the little deli by the golden seahorse fountain. Their conversation was wonderful, yet far from accepting his lonely-guy veneer at face value, Chelsea flashed him a conspiratorial grin.

"Except I've heard about you," she said. "You, sir, have a reputation. Did you know certain ladies in the building consider you a heartbreaker?"

He smiled and shrugged. "There's no such thing as bad press, right? I don't know. Not everyone's interested in hearing people can change."

Lunch at the deli turned into an entire afternoon. It was an amazing day—they both decided to blow off work, chatting by the fountain till the sunlight cast stark city shadows on the rippling water. They found themselves so engrossed in one another they decided to get dinner the next night, and then once more on the weekend, a Vietnamese meal, after which she promptly invited him up to her apartment.

"You don't know how amazing it is to find you," he told her. "I feel like I've known you for years."

"Yeah, me too," she said. "Tell me it's not too good to be true."

At work the next day, Alec found himself daydreaming about her. The smell of her perfume, her sense of humor. She adopted bad foreign accents when she was joking around, liked the color yellow because she felt it was generally underrepresented as a pigment.

"It's chemical, Albert," Alec said. He sat in his cubicle staring at his laptop screen as talk radio played softly from the desk of a neighbor. "There's just something about her. I feel like I'm home when she's around. Does that make sense?"

He turned his arm over so he could see Albert better. The swollen little man furrowed his brow, and rather than lending a supportive voice, he reminded Alec he'd been screwing around at work too much lately.

Alec sat back in his office chair. Purple 3D word art scrolled slowly across the laptop screen. It read, *Four Heads, Two Hearts.*

"I think I'm falling for her," he said.

"Ah, geeze," said Albert. "I knew you'd say that."

"But you don't sound happy about it."

"Listen, I'm not exactly what you'd call a lady's man. Point of fact, I'm not a man at all. I'm an arm tumor. I'm your arm tumor. It's just I don't want to see you get hurt, sport."

* * * * *

Alec stood at the stove in his kitchen as fragrant red spaghetti sauce simmered away in the pot. They'd been seeing each other a few weeks now, and things were going well enough he didn't mind cooking for her.

As he stirred in some salt and pepper, the phone in his pocket rang. He swore and answered it with a flourish.

"Hello? This is Alec."

The woman on the other end told him she was from a local news station, one which had picked up their story and wanted to air it on television.

"I'm sorry, how'd you hear about us?" he asked.

"One of your co-workers filled us in," she said. Husky voice, a bit like Kathleen Turner. "I have the name here somewhere. You're a fascinating couple. That was pretty clear."

"Yeah, but we're a strange couple, aren't we?" he said

"Alec—may I call you Alec? It's the twenty-first century, Alec. People are opening their minds out there. Non-traditional marriages, illicit drug legalization. We'd compensate you fully, of course. We'd love to meet you, and to be perfectly honest, we think our viewers would, too."

* * * * *

Chelsea scooped some sauce and layered it onto her pasta. She angrily plucked a piece of garlic bread from the loaf and jabbed at the air with her fork.

"Are you kidding me?" she said. "Why on earth did you say yes?"

Alec swallowed a bite. "Because it seemed like a good idea?"

Albert hiccupped and chirped, "Hell yes, it's a good idea! More scotch, please."

Alec took a sip from his icy, perspiring glass. He grimaced because of flavor more than burn.

"It's a bad idea because you didn't talk to me about it first," Chelsea said.

"But we'll have fun," Alec assured her. "Plus we get paid."

Her other head, Denise, snorted. She was good at that. Snort. Derision. Snort, snort. Like an anteater.

"It's a bad idea," she said, "because not everyone enjoys the limelight."

"You mean you don't enjoy it," said Albert.

Denise sneered at him. "You people do understand we're freaks, don't you? Of the four of us, which two cannot hide the fact we share a body with someone else?"

"Denise, it's the twenty-first century," said Alec. "People are opening their minds out there. Did you know you can gay marry your uncle in Colorado *and* smoke pot at the reception?"

Chelsea groaned, "You can be so dumb."

"Yeah, but not boring," said Alec. "Come on, Chels, it'll be fun. I haven't steered us wrong yet, have I?"

* * * * *

That Sunday morning, he drove them all down to the TV station on the north side of the city. An hour for hair and makeup, quick prep and run-through, and then they sat down on set in large yet uncomfortable leather chairs, Studio B, KKDO News Channel 11.

"Alec, Chelsea," the interviewer said. Her face was far too tan, her teeth a radioactive shade of white. "Can you reflect for us how hard it's been?"

"How do you mean?" said Chelsea. Alec couldn't help but notice how her skin glowed in the brilliant studio lights.

"Well the second heads," said the interviewer, "don't they make things difficult, you know, for your ... intimacy?"

Alec and Chelsea shared a glance.

"Occasionally," said Chelsea, "but Albert and Denise are parts of us. They're like extra limbs or knees you don't need but can't live without, you know what I mean?"

"No, I guess I don't," said the interviewer. She pointed at Denise with the tip of her pen. "That head there looks angry. Is that normal for it?"

"Pardon?" said Denise.

"Oh my goodness!" the interviewer laughed. "How on earth did you teach it to talk, Chelsea? Did it come naturally, or did you have to use people food?"

Silence filled the studio, an absence of sound so unqualified the noise that came after seemed to split the room in half.

"Ha!" said a gruff little voice.

Denise's face contorted with rage. Her lip quivering, she screamed, "Shut up, Albert!"

She raved like a lunatic on the car ride home. All afternoon, too, and the rest of the week. At bedtime on Friday, she finally admitted, "I want to sue them. That's what I want."

"The woman lost her job, Denise," Albert said. "You really want to pick on someone who already got what was coming to her?"

"What was coming? What was coming! Ha! I'll tell her when she's gotten what's coming."

"You're such a blowhard. All bark and no bite," Alec complained.

"Don't antagonize her, Alec," said Chelsea. She looked frustrated, exhausted, fed up. "Albert, Denise, pipe down, the both of you. Go to bed. We are all going to bed. No more talking."

But Alec couldn't sleep. Not a wink. Yellow street lights made window blind shadow razors on the bedroom ceiling. He stared at them in the darkness. Distant cars passed down the freeway ... Sounded like hissing serpents.

Albert slept under the blanket, sawing logs on his arm. For Chelsea, sleep seemed restless and shallow.

"I know what you're thinking, superstar."

Alec jerked at the sound of Denise's voice. His eyes locked with hers. She wasn't sleeping either. How long had she been staring at him?

"Thought you were asleep," he said.

"Did you?" said Denise. "Well that's the thing about guardians, Alec. We are sleepless. You're such a charmer, aren't you? Not precisely relationship material, though."

Alec frowned. "What are you talking about?"

"My girl likes you, but I think we both know it's only a matter of time until you screw this up, right? Just like you screwed up all those other relationships? Get out while you still can, Alec. Life can be sweet, or it can be a living nightmare. You choose, superstar."

"Are you threatening me?" Alec said.

"I don't know, am I?" and then she hawked a wad of phlegm and spat it into his eye. It clung to his upper eyelid. Alec groaned with disgust.

Chelsea startled awake. "Wha? Was goin' on?"

"Oh dear, did he wake you?" Denise said. "How inconsiderate of him. Alec, please, for the sake of your relationship, think of Chelsea's needs at least now and then."

"Get fucked, you awful Nazi lab experiment!" said

Alec.

"Hey, hey, watch the language," Chelsea said. "Was goin' on? Why're you two bickering?"

"I heard the whole thing, Chelsea," Albert said from beneath the blanket. "Nasty woman! I knew she had it in for him."

"She threatened me," Alec said. "Chelsea, the old hag threatened me."

"Oh Jesus. Grow a pair, Alec," Denise said.

"Can't he just borrow yours?" said Albert.

"All right, all right, that's enough," said Chelsea. She flipped on her bedside lamp, sat up straight, and ran her hands through her hair in frustration.

"Chels, babe—" Alec began.

"Kinda don't want to call me babe right now, okay? We need to talk about some things, Alec. I ... I don't know if this is working anymore."

* * * * *

Albert convinced Alec to drink enough scotch he'd forget his own name. It was only 5:22 AM, so Alec figured there was also plenty of time before breakfast to forget high school, his first sexual encounter, and of course, all traces of a girl named Chelsea.

"Sport, happy days will come again," said Albert.

"Why're m' underwear on m' head?"

"You said your head was cold."

"Why's m' ass cold?"

Eventually, the scotch dried up and Alec regained the ability to form cogent thoughts. He asked Albert to explain, just one more time, perhaps more clearly, why his girlfriend had left him.

"I think she's scared," Albert said. "She says she can't be with someone who's not supportive of her choices, which I guess means her choice to have the severed head of a raging bitch surgically grafted to her shoulder. Still, seems like an excuse to me. She loves you, Alec, but Denise is like her mom now. She's scared of love, scared of losing it. She's pushing you away, or, you know, allowing Denise to do it for her."

Alec considered this. He sat back in his arm chair and raised the empty scotch bottle to the red morning light silhouetting skyscrapers out the window.

"Well shit," he said. "Who the hell is scared of love?"

"Oh, you know, everybody on planet Earth," Albert said. "I'm only three years old, right? But I gotta tell you, sport, you've taught me a lot about the ugly side of love. Not to kick you when you're down, but there was a time you couldn't even remember how many girls you'd slept with in a year."

"That's not me anymore."

"I know it isn't. I also know you like this woman more than you've liked any other. Sport, you've got a choice here. She ran from you, which means you're free and clear and can run off yourself. Or, just maybe, you decide to get brave."

"You don't think I'm brave enough?" Alec said.

"Kinda beside the point, if you really need to know," said Albert. "Question is, do you think you're brave?"

* * * * *

Chelsea was a pro, a woman on the job, crunch numbers, build budget reports. Email, fax, remote drives; duplicate, triplicate; ergonomic PC suits and little golden name placards on rows of cubicles like vast, unending honeycombs.

Business as usual. Focus on the task at hand. Just pretend that guy, that Alec guy, pretend he doesn't even exist.

"Alec's an ass," said Denise. "Trust me, dear, men like him are a dime a dozen."

Chelsea sighed. She chewed on the disintegrating remains of a red rollerball pen.

"You know that's not true," she said. "He's one of a kind, just like me."

Denise smiled benevolently. "Dear, I married and divorced four men. Some were smart, others dumb. Half were incredible in the sack, and one was so bad he'd get his two minute jollies then roll over—"

A tennis ball flew across the office, over cubicle

walls, and hit Denise in the face.

"Ouch!" she said.

Another came, and then another. Each hit Denise, and after three, Chelsea stood and removed her from line-of-fire.

"The hell?" she said.

Across the office, near the back door the smokers always kept propped open, Alec stood behind a tennis ball machine. He fed in a ball. It flew and bounced off the back of Chelsea's chair.

"Alec?" said Chelsea. "What the hell are you doing?"

"What's it look like he's doing?" said Denise. "Being an abject ass, as usual."

"This one's for you, Chels," Alec said. He fed in a special white ball. It popped and flew, sailing across the office. Chelsea caught it in both hands. She rolled it over, noticed it was wrapped in paper.

"What's this?" she laughed. Co-workers and managers stood from their desks. "You're making a scene, Alec."

"Just read it for me, okay?"

Chelsea scowled at him but read all the same.

Dear girl of my dreams,
Four heads are better than one.
One heart is better than two.

Just try to run away from this.

Below this was a science news article copied and printed off Google.

Chelsea narrowed her eyes. "This ... is this real? Alec, is this real?"

"Yup," Alec said.

"Yup," chirped a gruff little voice.

"Dear, they can't be serious," said Denise. "Why on Earth would you think of such a thing?"

Chelsea shook her head. She grinned, and then she burst out laughing. "You're a madman, Alec!"

Alec grinned back. "Nah, I'm just really good with Google."

* * * * *

The world's first four-way/one-way wedding was a resounding success.

At a beautiful, dark wood-inlayed altar, Father Thompkins said, "Do you, Alec, take Chelsea?"

"I do."

"Do you, Chelsea, take Alec?"

"Yes, with all my heart."

"Alec, do you take Albert?" said their priest.

"Yes."

"Albert, do you take Chelsea?"

Albert made an assertive clicking sound with his tongue. "Uh-huh, I sure do, father."

"Alec, do you take Denise?"

"Erm...."

Denise glowered at him. "Say yes, you ass, this was your idea."

"Fine. Yes."

"Albert, do you take Chelsea?"

"Didn't we already do that one?" Chelsea asked.

"What?"

"I think we already did that one."

"Oh," said the father, "Right, um.... Chelsea, do you take...? Let's see ... do you take...?"

"Get on with it, Pope Francis!" Denise bellowed.

"Jeeze, all right," said the father. "Chelsea, do you ... You know what? How about this? Let's just leave it there. I now pronounce you man and wife and man and wife. You may now all kiss each other ... if something like that is even possible."

They all kissed, there at the altar under the eyes of the Lord. Also a success: the procedure which grafted Alec's head to Chelsea's right shoulder and Albert's head to her left forearm. They were four heads, but one body, one soul now. Bound together for all time, in both the physical and marital sense.

"Do you guys think this is getting weird?" Albert said between long, awkward kisses.

"Good thing we didn't invite our families," said Alec. The preacher crossed himself and quickly stepped away from the altar.

"Love you, babe," said Alec, "forever and ever. No more running or being afraid."

It took them several tries to get in the car. Took more than several to explore the art of single-body, four-head lovemaking.

"Chelsea, I still don't believe," said Denise as they shared a honeymoon cocktail on a golden beach in Maui. The sky was so blue and the clouds so small and vague.

"I know you don't believe, Denise," said Chelsea. "But that's okay. I understand more about life and love than you know. Our husbands, I really think they're starting to grow on me. You know what I mean? They're starting to grow on me. Get it?"

Denise frowned at her. "Perfectly hilarious, I am sure."

And they all lived happily ever after, or as close to it as human beings manage to get.

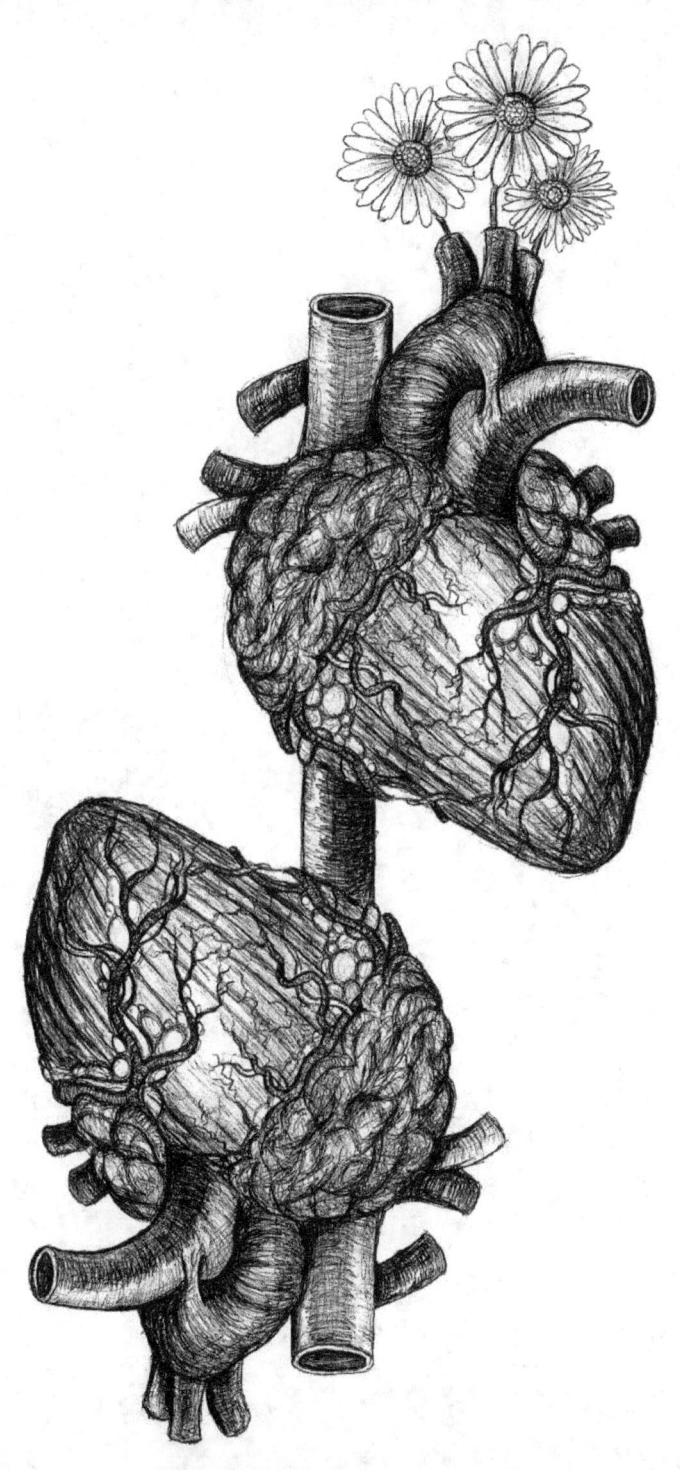

Welcome to your mid-life crisis.
My name is Archibald Pendragon.
Don't mind the guns.
Or the hounds.
Or my collection of bear and demon traps.

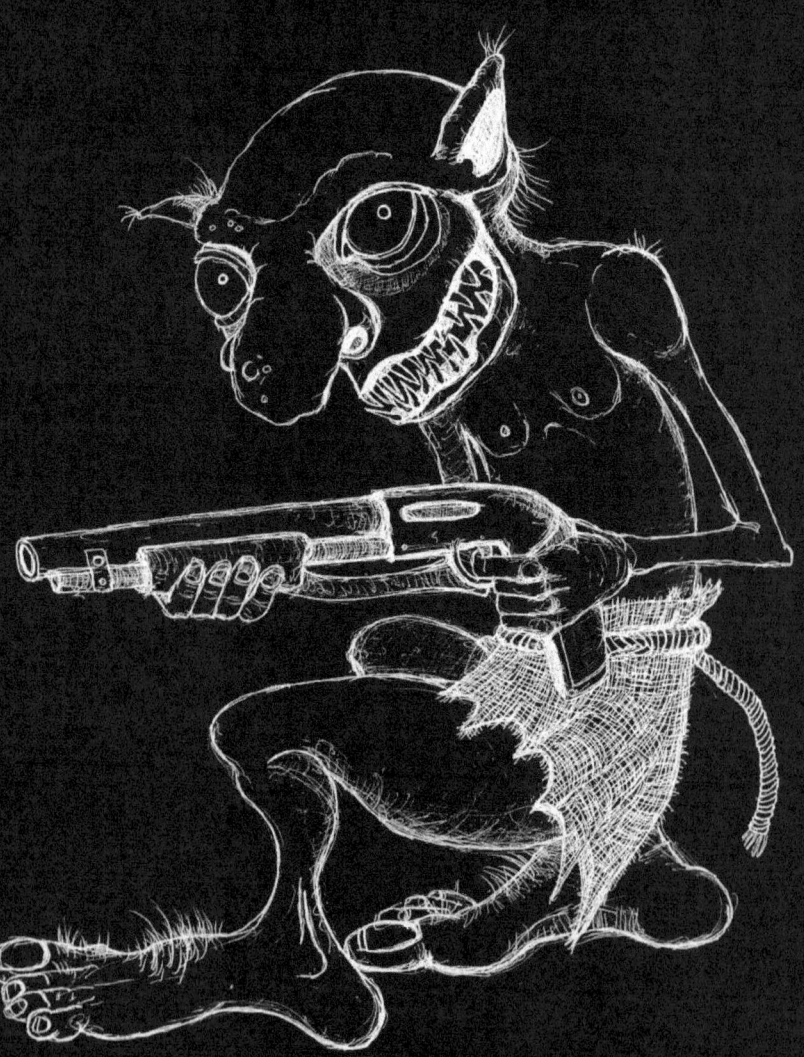

MID-LIFE CRISIS: THE VIDEO GAME

PRESS start to begin.

Select your character.

You have selected <u>Overweight Adulterer</u>.

Game commencing....

......

{Welcome to your mid-life crisis. My name is Archibald Pendragon. Don't mind the guns. Or the hounds. Or my collection of bear and demon traps. Pull up a chair, traveler. I can see you're weary from the road.}

Press X to sit by Archibald's roaring fire.

{There, that's better. Cold bones are aching bones. Tell me what troubles you, my friend.}

Headset support enabled. Tell Archibald what troubles you.

"My wife kicked me out last week."

{I'm sorry to hear that. But you're in luck. Old Archibald Pendragon happens to be a world-class wife and husband slayer.}

Please state your gender now.

"Male."

You have just said <u>male</u>. Is that correct?

"Yes."

Verified. You are a <u>male</u>. You mentioned you have a <u>wife</u>. Is that correct?

"Yes."

Did you just say <u>yes</u>?

"Yes."

Are you sure you have a <u>wife</u>?

"Yes, damnit, I have a ... well, no ... I guess I'm not sure anymore."

Verified. You have a <u>husband</u>.

"What?"

Game commencing.

{So you need old Archibald to slay your husband, eh?}

"No, I have a wife."

Command not recognized.

{I know I don't look like much, traveler. Maybe I've seen a few too many winters and these trembling, arthritic hands of mine mean my best days are behind me. But don't you count me out just yet. Let's go slay a husband, yes?}

"Wife."

Command not recognized.

Press X to select Archibald's white winged Hunter Pegasus and begin your journey.

{Very well then, traveler. Away, my mighty Pegasus!}

Press Y to smell the rain on the wind and enjoy the rolling, verdant landscape filling all the world below you.

{My gods, what a sight. Tell me, traveler, how long have you known your husband?}

"My wife. I've known her twenty-four years."

{Ah, a lifer, are ye? Heh. Let me guess, you and your man have grown apart recently.}

"Well yeah, we have. I mean no, that's not why she kicked me out. I can acknowledge I did wrong. I know I screwed up big time. But damnit, she drove me to it."

{I hope you don't mind my saying, traveler, but your husband is a blind fool for letting you go. And if I'm not too much mistaken ... Look, do you see it? That cave set into yonder mountain? The troll dwells there.}

"What do you mean troll?"

{Why your husband, of course. May his eyes grow dim, and his bones shatter, and his penis shrivel and turn black as the ashes of a diseased dire viper.}

Do you wish to enter the cave and confront your spouse?

"Yes."

Are you sure you wish to enter the cave?

"Why not? It's not like she'll actually be in there."

Username CutiePie109 has entered the game. She says, "Wow, look at these graphics. That Overweight Adulterer character looks just like my husband."

"Heather? Is that you?"

CutiePie109 says, "Oh my god, Alex? What the hell are you doing in my game?"

"What the hell are you doing in mine?"

{Good, I'm glad the pair of ye are still itching for a fight. Here's a shotgun for you, and for you, sir, a matching shotgun.}

CutiePie109 says, "Did he just call me sir?"

"Hold on, hold on. I am not going to have a gun battle with my wife."

{But you must. That's how these things get settled. Either you slay the troll, or the troll slays you.}

"She's not a troll! And maybe we're on the outs right now, but that doesn't mean we want to hurt each other."

CutiePie109 says, "Speak for yourself, you lousy

cheat!"

Press B to dodge <u>CutiePie109's</u> headshot.

Shot dodged.

Press right trigger to slay <u>CutiePie109</u>.

"This is silly, Heather."

<u>CutiePie109</u> says, "Is it?"

"Look, I can only say I'm sorry so many times."

Press B to dodge behind the nearest needling stalagmite.

"Jesus!"

<u>CutiePie109</u> has blown the stalagmite to pieces. Press A to lie prone. Press right trigger to slay CutiePie109.

"No! I'm not going to slay my wife."

<u>CutiePie109</u> says, "You still don't get it, do you, Alex? I wasn't allowed to bother you about the weight you gained. But the second I'm not as fit as I used to be, all bets are off and you go sleep with the office whore."

"Baby, listen—"

<u>CutiePie109</u> says, "You don't get to call me baby. Pull the trigger, big man."

"I don't want to pull it."

Press right trigger to slay <u>CutiePie109</u>.

{You must pull the trigger, traveler. It's over. Your husband isn't going to take you back.}

"I don't believe that. Not for a second."

<u>CutiePie109</u> says, "See? This is what I'm talking about. He's right, Alex. I'm not taking you back. Now lie still."

Press B to dodge—

Your head has been blown to pieces.

Game over.

Would you like to play again?

Press start to begin.

Select your character.

You have selected <u>Neutered Apologist</u>.

"Maybe if I tell her I'm sorry one more time...."

Are you sure you want to apologize? Are you really sure?

Our little black and gray cat stood on his hind legs, shaking his hips and performing kitty-sized air guitar.

THE FALL AND RISE OF MAX ZIGGY

Originally appeared in Penumbra eMag, April 2012

WE brought the cat home from the animal shelter, named him Max Ziggy after my favorite musician. The real Max Ziggy had died in a bathtub on Sunset Strip soon before our Max was born. Overdose. Go figure.

The cat was cute enough. I'm more of a dog person, myself.

"Please, Dad," Patrick had said, "I really want a kitty."

Max played with little toy mice and danglers and a laser pointer, all the usual cat stuff. But then one

Saturday afternoon I decided to put on my favorite Max Ziggy and the Known Criminals album: *Buzzkill Blues*.

"Here you go," I said to Patrick, "this is better than your kid bands on TV."

The bass kicked in, the drums beat, the singer wailed, and Max Ziggy's legendary minor pentatonic solo filled our living room.

Patrick stuck out his tongue. "I like my kid bands better."

"You just have to know how to move to it. Watch."

I stood in front of the stereo, slung my left hand out at my side and formed my right into a pick-holding claw: classic air guitar positioning. I closed my eyes, flexed my fingers against the phantom fret board, shook my hips, and let the solo fly.

Patrick laughed. I smiled and opened one eye to find him staring across the room. Our little black and gray cat stood on his hind legs, shaking his hips and performing kitty-sized air guitar.

"I'll be damned," I said.

We played another song for him, and another, and the cat soloed his heart out, slinking his paws back and forth, sliding and picking.

"Maybe he can play real guitar, too," said Patrick.

It was an interesting thought. I played guitar back

in high school, still had an old Martin acoustic lying around in the attic. I dug it out, tuned it up, and placed it in front of Max. He looked down at it, up at me, and began to bathe himself.

Patrick frowned. "I guess he doesn't. Are you sure it's in the right keys?"

"Strings, son. Guitars have strings."

"Well, maybe you have to play the music again."

I shrugged and put on track six of *Buzzkill*. The drums rode 4/4; the bass sped double time. Max nodded his head, tapped the rhythm on the floor, sat back onto his hind legs. The human Max Ziggy let fly another solo. Feline Max paused. He tilted his head and stared at the speakers. He began to shake, to writhe. He let out a high meow and jumped onto the guitar. His back paws struck the strings, while his front danced over the fret board. It was note perfect, not a pluck out of place.

I turned the stereo off, but Max just kept playing. He knew the song, inside and out.

"This cat doesn't just have Max Ziggy's name," I said. "He *is* Max Ziggy."

"Cool. What do we do now?"

I thought for a moment. "I didn't get very far with my band in high school. I can't tell you about record deals or recording studios or international jetsetting. I do know one thing, though: start small but think big.

That meant dances and talent shows when I was a kid, but these days, it's all about open mic nights."

"Open mic? What's that?"

"It's like a real gig. Only you don't get paid, you only play a few songs, and people don't actually pay attention to you."

"People don't pay attention? What's the point of that?"

"No one really knows, son. Besides, playing for people is all about the music."

"All about the music?"

"That's right, and nobody can ignore a guitar-playing cat. Now, I've heard that Rascal's Bar has an open mic Saturday nights. It's on the other side of town, somewhere. Let's see."

I pulled out my phone and got the bar's address.

"Here it is."

Max chattered and leapt from his guitar. He jumped onto my arm, made me drop the phone, followed it to the floor and pressed buttons on its face.

"Bad Maxy!"

I shooed him away and picked up the phone to see that Max had somehow sent a text.

"Aw," I said, "he copied and pasted the address. I hope whoever gets it is smarter than a cat."

* * * * *

We went to Rascal's later that night, Max and I, just us and his guitar. A guy called Dave was running the PA system. He took a good look at Max in his pet carrier and sniffed. "I'm allergic, man."

"But he can play. I mean, he can really play."

"That ain't the question. Cats just aren't sanitary, man."

Max meowed. He scratched and bit at the carrier.

I pointed down at him. "Be careful what you say. This cat here happens to be the reincarnation of Max Ziggy himself."

Dave sniffed again. "Primo, man. Wicked."

Max howled. People in the bar started to look our way.

"You don't believe me? I'll prove it."

I pulled the guitar out of its case, laid it on the floor, put the pet carrier down.

"Okay, Max," I said, "do your thing."

I opened the carrier's door. Max sprung out, right past the guitar and up Dave's pant leg.

"Shit, man!" said Dave.

Max clawed his way up, into Dave's leather coat. He dug around for a moment, and then he pulled back. He clenched a glass vial full of white powder in his teeth.

"My stash!" said Dave.

Max jumped and ran under a table. We ran after

him, but it was too late. Max howled and shivered; a dusting of the powder covered his little black nose.

Dave looked pretty upset, but before he could scream at me, Max stumbled to the guitar and climbed atop it. He played the title track of *Love Thief*, the ballad. It was pure beauty. Barflies and waitresses and even the bartender turned to look at him. They waved their hands in the air. They sung along and held lighters above their heads. Magical. Even Dave got swept up in it.

Halfway through Max's set, a pinstripe-suited, slick-haired gentleman approached me.

"You this cat's owner?" he said.

"Why yes sir, I am."

"He plays just like Max Ziggy."

"Well, that's no coincidence. This cat here happens to be the reincarnation of Max himself."

The gentleman passed his tongue over his teeth. "Is that a fact?"

"Yes sir, it is."

"I happen to have known Max Ziggy. He was a close, personal friend of mine. In fact, I managed him for sixteen years. His tragic and untimely death was a real blow to me. Now tell me, what could possibly make you think that this cat and my old friend are one and the same?"

I thought for a moment and scratched my head.

"He plays a lot like him."

"I see cats do crazy shit on the internet all the time."

"Well ... when he plays, he gets a faraway look in his eyes, like maybe he's made contact with nymphs from some magical realm, or like maybe he's communicating directly with God."

"Too much catnip."

I scratched my head once more, looked at Max, atop his guitar, fuzzy little paws flying. "You ever see a cat do that much coke and still able to play like Max Ziggy?"

"... You may have something there. He got any representation?"

"Well, he's registered with the Humane Society."

"No, I mean management. Is he under contract with anybody?"

I shook my head. He reached into his jacket and pulled free a glossy black business card.

"Give me a call sometime," he said. "Maybe we can do business. You do right by that cat, and he could be a big star someday."

He paused a moment, stared at Max. "It's the damndest thing. I was just passing through on my way back to L.A. when I get some weird text with this dive's address. I thought I'd show up and see who was pulling my leg. Damndest thing."

I raised an eyebrow, smiled and nodded. I didn't say a word.

* * * * *

Nose-bleed seats at my own cat's stadium rock concert.

"It's okay, Dad," said Patrick. "At least we can see him on the big TV screen."

Red carpets, clothing lines and roadies and state-of-the-art tour busses, large crystal bowls filled with just the yellows of the multicolored cat kibble. Max had it all.

And there he and his band were, on the JumboTron, playing for eighty-thousand, him astride his Les Paul, kicking and plucking, making a racket and scratching at the stage.

"Is he trying to smash the guitar?" said a guy behind me.

"Nah," said another, "I think he's just trying to bury it."

Tonight it was Denver, the night before it had been Phoenix, and the night before that had been the award show. The new Max Ziggy had won both best new artist and the lifetime achievement award. The whole world was in love with him.

"I think Max and I need to have a few words," I said.

After the show, we pushed past his adoring fans

trying to get paw-print autographs, past his personal spiritual advisor and past his body guards. We came to his dressing room. He lay on a mink cat bed, next to a white cat in a pink skirt and no top.

"Cover your eyes, son," I said.

A rotund little roadie opened a can of cat food, smeared it into a bowl, and split open a little white pill, emptying it of God knew what. He put it in front of Max, who ate greedily.

His manager entered, patted Patrick's head. "Good lookin' kid, good lookin' guy. Good lookin' fellows."

I smiled half-heartedly.

"Hell of a show," he said.

"Yeah, hell of a show."

"Listen, I've been meaning to talk to you. A certain self-titled debut album just went gonzo in Russia. Would you believe it?"

"Imagine that."

"Yeah, so anyways, I'm thinking this whole North American tour thing is great for little-pond swimmers, but our Maxy ain't no little-pond swimmer, am I right?"

I shook my head. "Another tour?"

"Bingo. I'm talking Maxemilian versus the Reds, I'm talking international sponsorship, I'm talking major rubles, you get me?"

"I don't know. I mean, he looks so worn out. He

hardly plays with his toys anymore, and I thought we were really going to get serious about rehab."

"Rehab?" said Max's manager. "For a cat? What, are you crazy? He's fine. It will all be fine. Hey, haven't I always taken care of us? Max is rich, I'm rich, and if I'm not too much mistaken, you're rich too, right?"

"Well ... yeah."

"Is he or is he not the reincarnation of *the* Max Ziggy? I mean, we got his spiritual advisor to verify it and tell the world. And ain't it just been success after success from then on?"

"Yeah ... and that's great and all. But ... isn't it supposed to be about the music?"

He stared me dead in the eye. He blinked once, and then twice. "Who told you a stupid thing like that?"

I thought for a moment, glanced over at Max. I looked at Patrick, looked at the way he stared at the drugged food Max was eating. I smiled, took the manager's hand and shook.

"I think we can do business."

He grinned.

"Tell you what," I said, "why don't you give me and the boy a few private minutes with Max? Don't you worry, I'll convince him."

Max's manager's grin broadened. "Sure," he said,

"C'mon, everybody out. That means you too, princess."

The white cat in the pink skirt followed everyone from Max's dressing room, leaving only Max, Patrick, and myself.

"I don't want him to tour anymore, Dad," said Patrick. "I miss giving him kitty treats and letting him climb under my sheets at night."

"Don't worry, son. There won't be another tour."

I crossed the room, put a hand out and patted Max's side. He glanced at me and cleaned the spot.

"Well, Max old boy," I said, "we've done and seen some crazy things. Traveled all over, played everywhere. But I think it's time to pull the plug."

Max continued to bathe.

"Understand I wouldn't dream of parting you from your success. I'm damn proud of you. We both are."

Max yawned.

"But you see, there's a sickness in this business. These people will just eat you up and make you do more and more and go faster and faster, until you have nothing left of what you started with. You've seen it all before, you know? Back when you were human. It did you in then, and it'll do you in now. Do you understand, Max? It's got to end. I think we all just need to go home."

Max stopped bathing. He looked me in the eyes, in that human way, that way which told he wasn't just my cat, but he was my friend too. He opened his mouth, as if to finally say he loved us and wanted nothing more than to just go home. It turned into another yawn. He stretched, lay his head down, and passed out cold.

"I guess he's really tired," said Patrick.

I glanced at Max's food dish. "Yeah, imagine that."

"What do we do now, Dad?"

"Only one thing to do, son."

I lifted Max gently and tucked him under my jacket. He never made a peep, not as we walked through the stadium, not as we made it to the car, and not until Denver was far behind us.

* * * * *

We sold the house, sold the cars, sold the jet tub and the flat screens and the white pool table. Broke Max's contract, got sued, but it ended in a mistrial. Apparently, managerial rights don't extend to death and reincarnation as a house pet. All that money Max earned paid for court costs. Gave half of what was left to charity, and I invested the rest for Patrick's future.

The three of us moved into a house very much like our old one. Nobody bothered us; nobody begged Max for paw-print autographs. Thanks to some nontoxic hair dye, he was orange now, so people didn't really recognize him, anyway. We put Max on a strict water and kibble detox program, and the good news was he hadn't chased the dragon in months.

We sat on the couch one day, Patrick and I, watching TV and petting our cat. A 'where are they now' style program came on, highlighting the New Max Ziggy and the Catnip Scavengers.

"Maybe we shouldn't watch this, Dad," said Patrick. "It might upset him."

"Yeah, maybe you're right."

I turned the TV off.

"Look at him, Dad. He looks so sad."

I gave max a good rub under his chin. "I know, son, but it really was for the best."

"Yeah. Hey, Dad, do you think, I mean, maybe for old time's sake?"

"The guitar? We'd better not, son."

"Not the guitar, Dad, not really." Patrick stood, crossed to the stereo. He picked out an album, my favorite, *Buzzkill Blues*. He smiled and gave it a spin.

The bass kicked in, the drums beat, the singer wailed, and Max Ziggy's legendary minor pentatonic solo filled our living room.

Our Max began to nod, to tap the rhythm on the couch. He rose onto his hind legs. He flexed his paw against the phantom fret board, shook his hips, and let the solo fly. I had to do the same.

Max, Patrick, and I played our hearts out, and when the album ended, we spun it again. It was really only about the music to us, anyway.

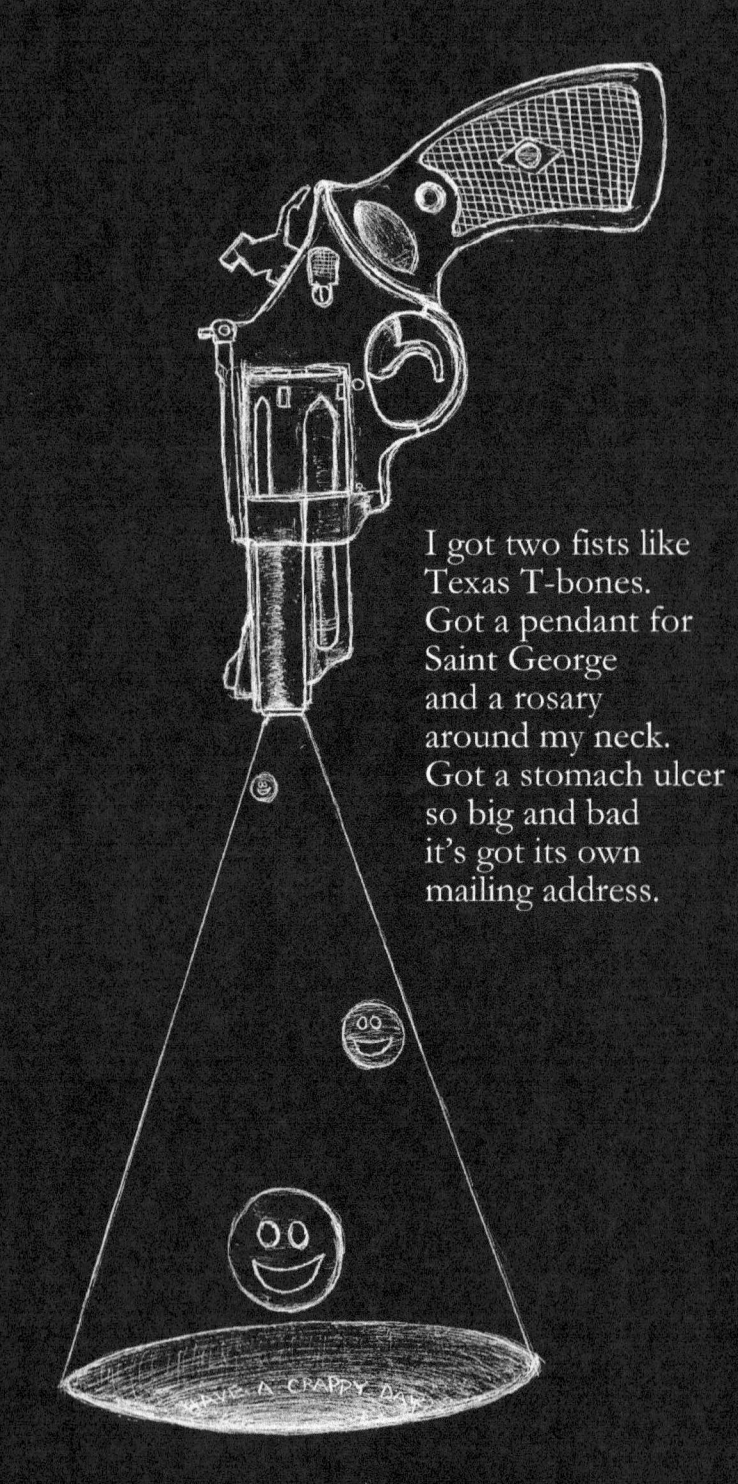

I got two fists like
Texas T-bones.
Got a pendant for
Saint George
and a rosary
around my neck.
Got a stomach ulcer
so big and bad
it's got its own
mailing address.

HAVE A CRAPPY DAY

JACK THE HAMMER'S ONLINE IDENTITY CRISIS

Originally appeared in Crime Syndicate Magazine, January 2016

{CLICK}

Welcome back to *mysecretdiary.com*, Jackson! Your personal online diary is open and ready for more secrets!

January 18

Mood: *sad*

Outlook: *cloudy with a chance of misery*

Jackson Palmer ain't my name no more. I realized that today, diary. Pissed me off royally. They been calling me Jack the Hammer for nearly twenty years. Twenty goddamn years! Frustrating. Infuriating. I fix problems for people. Pretty good at it, too. Least I used to be. Mafia, Triad, I don't judge. But what's a hard case like me to do when I'm the one in need of fixing?

Here's my secret for today, diary: I been doing this lousy work so long, I often forget there's places out there where nobody gets shot, or extorted, or wrapped up in garbage bags and dumped in the Hudson River.

You should see what they been saying about me over on thugieslist.com.

{CLICK}

Welcome to thugieslist.com, the world's premier consumer review site for mafia thugs, hit men, and muscle. You have selected to display the latest reviews for Hoboken, New Jersey's Jackson "Jack the Hammer" Palmer.

wiseguyforlife36

Jack the Hammer is a total joke. I used to like the guy. I used to respect him like crazy. But he's gone soft. There just ain't no getting through to the guy. I specifically told him to keep an eye out.

"Jack," I says to him. "You stay in the car and keep an eye out. Rosco and I will make the deal."

So me and my boy Rosco went to make the deal, only

the deal went south. They started shooting at us. We shot back. Rosco and I high-tailed it to the car.

"What the shit is this?" says Rosco.

Shit you not, Jack the Hammer was napping behind the wheel! You believe that? KEE-RIST!

One star for services NOT rendered!

college*grad*mike

gradulated comunity college with Jack. hlped me improv my english, He's an ok dood I guess. but I hav to say, the guys lost his edge. Same dood worked muscle for Boss DiMaggio for 17 yers. Imagine that guy going soFt! Its like he dont care no more. Not a profeshinal. Real slippery eel. and have you sen his face LaTeley? Talk about an major SKIN CONDITION!   2   stars.

{CLICK}

Welcome back to *mysecretdiary.com*, Jackson!

Diary,

I got two fists like Texas T-bones. Got a pendant for Saint George and a rosary around my neck. Got a stomach ulcer so big and bad it's got its own mailing address.

Had to work over Ricky the Rat today. Poor old Rick was a broken, bloody wad of hamburger before I was through with him. I brought him down to the meat plant 'cause the boss said to tenderize him.

He cried, "Don't hit me no more, Jack!" and, "Not in the face! Mother of chicken lasagna, not in the goddamn face!"

But I couldn't help myself. Used to have better control, you know?

"Look at you!" I said. "Bet you think you look better than me, Rick. So damn handsome. So debonair. I got a skin condition, understand?" I socked him in the eye. "I got a skin condition!" I slammed his head into a big suspended steer carcass.

"Awwwwooooow! You're crazy, man! You're fucking crazy! You look fine!"

Horse shit! Most people're so flashy. Know what I'm saying? So damn flashy and sassy. And me. Look at me. Grade A, prime-cut loser. With a side of special loser sauce. And loser steak fries. So you can dip the fries into the …

Ah, what does it matter?

I worked old Ricky over pretty good. Too good, actually. The boss gets one good look at him and says, "I can't use him like this. Poor bastard ought to be in traction."

I could'a been a doctor, you know? Or even like a politician. Governor Palmer. Senator Palmer. The Hammer always got so much respect. But what if I don't want to be the Hammer no more? Ah, hell, what if I don't even know *who* the Hammer is?

Incoming message from friendtracker.com instant messaging

{CLICK}

—Jackson? Are you online?

Yeah.

—Payment didn't come through, Jackson.

Jesus, doc, you know I'm good for it.

—I know you've been good for it in the past. I also know you're having an existential meltdown at the moment.

So what if I am?

—Jackson, we've talked about this. Anger is always healthy. But what do we say about rage?

Come on, doc . . .

—Jackson, reinforcement is key. It really is. What do we say about rage?

You can't spell *discourage* without *rage*.

—And?

You also can't spell *discourage* without *disco*.

—And?

Disco is the prefix of both *disconnect* and *discord*.

—And?

Christ, doc, I gotta tell you, it gets fuzzy for me after that.

—Hmph. That figures. Where the fuck's my money,

Jackson?

Yeesh. I'll get it to you.

—Huh?

I said I'll get it to you. Next week. All right? Fair enough? Aren't psychiatrists supposed to be, you know, more nurturing than this?

—Perhaps. Most psychiatrists don't pay alimony to three different women, though. Good afternoon, Jackson. Onward towards mental stability!

{CLICK}

I think the doc means business this time, diary. I wonder how my cash reserve situation is looking.

{CLICK}

First Bank of Hoboken Online Branch: we are open and ready to serve you, Jackson.

Checking: $4.21

Savings: $0.02

We notice your funds are a bit low. Consider applying for a personal loan today!

{CLICK}

Note to self, *sigh*

{CLICK}

Welcome back to *thugieslist.com*. Previously viewed

profile loaded.

DarthToughGuy

Hang on, hang on, hang the frig on. You guys want to tell me you've got nothing good to say about old Jack? Nothing at all? Hell, man, I'll go to the mat for him. I'll go to the mat for him all day long. Maybe's the guy's lost his edge—and I ain't saying he ain't—but whatever's bothering him right now, he'll get it sorted out. Trust me. I grew up with Jack. Some'a youse *wise guys* know that ;-)

He was a good kid, man. Good to his mom, good to his friends and his baby sister. He was smart. Real smart. I mean, his dad was a loser—put the belt to the poor guy, oh, three, four times a week—but I really do think Jack's done well to make the best of a bad situation. How many of you bellyachers has this man bent over backwards for? How many times, whether you invited him to or not, has he bailed your assess out and pulled your scorching nutsacks from the proverbial fire?

When the boss says push a button on a guy, good old Jackie pushes the button. When the boss says take out that armored car containing kilo after glorious kilo of White Bunk, hell, man, he's the only guy on the job don't powder his own nose. We go way back, Jackie and me. He's never let me down. At least, he never used to.

college*grad*mike

earth to *DarthToughGuy*: Up yours, DINGUS LICKER! I don't give a holy SHIZ whts "bothering" Jack. darth, plese. the guys a expert screw up! I wus with him the other day, Freakshow started crying in the middle of Dr. Hoo. I mean, we wer just sitting there, watching Dr. Hoo, and the looser starts bawlin like a little girl! I askd him what was wrong and all, Jack just wipes his eyes and says, "watch you're fcking Dr. Hoo! Stop asking so many stoopid fcking questions!"

Fcker totoally ruined BBC nite with THE DOCTOR! Wht a jerk! My 2 star review has been downgraded to a very pissed off 1 STAR!

{CLICK}

Welcome to *jobfisher.com*! Reinvigorate your life with a new career from *JobFisher* today!

Search listings for: "thug" AND "hired gun" AND "gentle heart" AND "good with children"

Searching . . .

No jobs found.

{CLICK}

DarthToughGuy

Listen here, *college*grad*mike*, you don't know jack about Jack!

*college*grad*mike*
I know he shits all ovr Dr. Hoo! Thats what I know!

{CLICK}
I just can't understand where my life went off the rails, diary.

Yeah, I cry. Ain't no shame in that. Show me a guy who don't cry at all, and I'll show you a real cold fish. My old man never cried. Not in front of me, anyhow. I am absolutely convinced he never shed a single tear in his life, neither.

I'm drinking too much. Maybe that's the problem. What was that country song from back in the day? Beer full'a tears or some crap? Something like that? Don't know. Don't care.

Hey, I got reasons to cry, all right? I got some shit wrong with my life. And I don't just cry every once in a while. I cry a lot. More than a lot. I cry all the damn time. I'm a wreck. I'm a time bomb. I'm a—

Hold on. Pizza's here.

. . . . . .

You see what I mean? You see how I just demolished that entire pizza by myself? Who the fuck does that? 'Cept fer like chicks on the rag and super fat dudes and—

Aw, man, what the fuck is wrong with me!

Incoming message from *friendtracker.com* instant messaging

{CLICK}

—Jackson, it's your psychiatrist again. 2nd wife late on Jaguar payment. Next week not soon enough. Going to need that money from you, guy. Pay up.

{CLICK}

DarthToughGuy

Hey, *college*grad*mike*, go fuck yourself! How 'bout that, wise-ass? Go fuck yourself, you fucking SKIN FLUTE GUZZLER!

college*grad*mike

Hey, fck you, pal! Fck you and fck you're fcking hole lcking stupid fck face!

DarthToughGuy

Really? That's nice. Umm, how old are you?

college*grad*mike

the Fck dose it matter how fcking old I am?! Old enogh to stick a fcking candelabra up your fcking ace and lite it on fire with a fcking WWII flame throwr!

{CLICK}

Stop, STOP, *STOP!*

It's too much craziness, diary. It's too much insanity. Is a little peace and calm too hard to come by these days? Is catching just one goddamn break every now and then?

When I was kid, man, oh, I had everything figured out. I knew what the world was. Better yet, I knew who *I* was. How come I was so much wiser then? How come I feel so stupid now?

I'm forty-nine years old. I have no children. I have no significant other. Hell, man, most of the time I don't even have a proper pad to crash at. I had chances to be happy. I had shots at the golden mile. But I blew 'em. Each and every last one of them. I feel ugly. I feel old. I hate myself so much it's hard to breathe sometimes.

Ugh.

I guess you don't understand.

'Cause you're just a stupid online diary.

And I substitute you for actual human companionship.

And I'm acting like some lovesick-puppy sixteen-year-old girl

Ugh.

Well that's it. That's decided. No more fucking around. Here we go.

{CLICK}

Welcome to jobfisher.com! Search listings for "entry level" AND "on-job training" AND "good with children" AND

{CLICK}

No, no, you know what, diary?

{CLICK}

Welcome to partyoftwo.com, the hottest spot for relationship hunting on the WWW!
Search for: "40's-something" AND "warm personality" AND "generous spirit" AND

{CLICK}

No, that's not it either, diary. A chick is the last thing I need right now. I know what I have to do. I know how to get my life back on track.

{CLICK}

First Bank of Hoboken Online Branch: consider applying for a personal loan today!
{CLICK}
You have selected **Apply for a Personal Loan**. Do

you wish to continue?

{CLICK}

. . . Processing . . .

. . . Processing . . .

Personal loan approved! Congratulations, Jackson!

{CLICK}

Doc, are you still there?

—I am

Good

—You got my money?

Yeah, doc. Payment'll be on your way real soon.

{CLICK}

Welcome to contractkillers.net!

We make people disappear, capicé?™

Search for: "Hoboken" AND "psychiatrist hit" AND "money no object" AND "make it hurt"

{CLICK}

You know something, diary? Maybe all I need is a little house cleaning. It's not like anybody'll be able to trace it back to me.

It all comes around. It all comes around, man. Where you been, Jackson? Where you been hiding? Just like that, diary, I am feeling much, much better

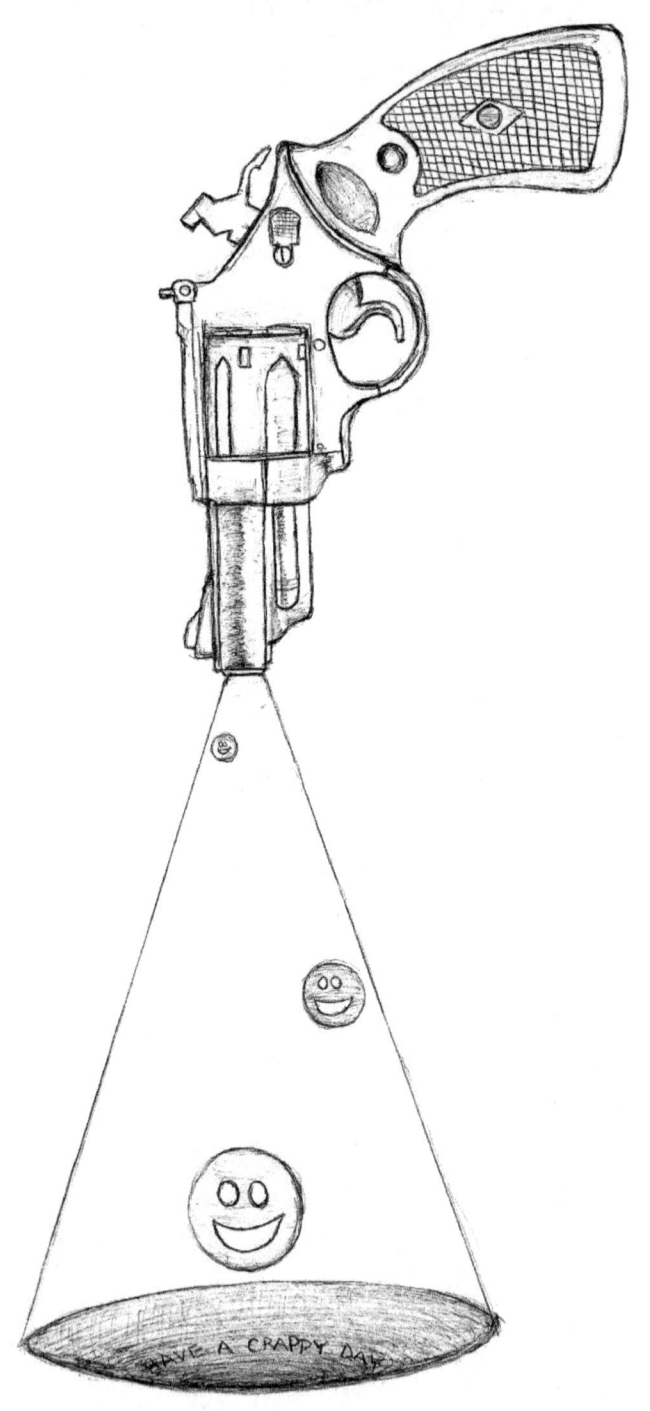

HAVE A CRAPPY DAY

ABOUT THE AUTHOR

JEFF BOWLES' work has appeared in some of the nation's top magazines and anthologies, such as PodCastle, Black Static, The Threepenny Review, and Spark: a Creative Anthology. He earned his Master of Fine Arts in Creative Writing at Western State Colorado University, where he studied under industry veterans and produced a horror fantasy novel entitled, Body of Heaven, Body of Darkness. Jeff currently lives in Southern Colorado, where he dreams strange dreams and spends far too much time out under the stars.